QUERENCIA

WINTER 2026

Querencia Press – Chicago Il

QUERENCIA PRESS
© Copyright 2026

ISBN

978 1 963943 52 8

www.querenciapress.com

First Published in 2026

**Querencia Press, LLC
Chicago IL**

Printed & Bound in the United States of America

CONTENTS

POETRY

White/Out

so I wake up and it's white out.
highway traffic is muted
by wind chimes, like when your mind
tries to misremember something.

I put on my good boots and coat
and walk into a cold which bites at me
like a years-long vice.

I don't know where I'm going;
just that I'm going somewhere
else.

so it's white out and snowflakes
are hitting me in both eyes—
little truth bombs from the sky,
little scythes to break my concentration.

    did you know there are different ways
    to move through every doorway?

some are portals. or dead ends.
or hallways lined with art that's lined
with clues on where to go next.

      do you understand yet?
      do you see how you've been missed?

none of this real.
it's a metaphor on a loop—

something bigger than me   or you   or us.

—Nicholas Olah (he/him)

Opening

Jejune days. Counting apples to slice.
Only roentgen rays can measure the bones
of this house.

We step down the fire ladder into reflective pools.
Deposit artifacts under the bus stop bench.

Asperse, asperse to the walls. He calls and calls,
then falls into a dead tooth slumber.

I return alone, an asterisk, and hunt for shoes.
The socks are sodden and torn.

No darning can mend this

time
        the split

too far.

—Jenny Bemjamin (she/her)

on auditing survival

The what and what-nots of survival
always lately leading
me to the question
        of who
      for who — whom
    with who — whom
        because of who

these questions
get treacherous sometimes
the litany for survival starts
to resemble a conditional,
        a conditioned suicide note.

if ______ then ______
if not ______ oh well ______
            t o o   b a d
and in circles
rinse, repeat,   r e s u r r e c t

is survival healthcare
            insurance and W2s and 401Ks
            what glory it has been in
the land of living
deads and why
must anyone want that fruit called survival?

is survival deep breaths
            and unruly exhales
            without permission
why does every second person willingly ingest pacemakers?

is survival the thickening
            impenetrability of blood
            baffling upsurge of
bloodthinner sales evidences a wasteland

and. and. and.

does survival guarantee
          and gestate the act
of surviving does it mean
survive does it mean to survive
a survival that is only
paradoxically won
that is only dying
breaths and death and that
is only witnessing dead
and death these days. Am i
surviving? Do i possess survival?

You asked me about survival
and surviving and
all i can do is speak
        of the
   to the   with the
        dead.

—SHRADDHA SHAH (she/they)

Black Cotton Gospel *(1999)*
—for Brent, always—K Road

The rugby boys
streaked across the field,
mud on their thighs,
and my stomach dropped—
arcade tokens never came back.

Short shorts—
Aotearoa's drag.
Black cotton.
Pink pride.
Field fame.
Homo shame—
the people's game.

Grass-stained piety.
Poly lads—
smiling in confession.
Hail Marys consumed whole
in shot glasses.

But here, beneath the neon choir of K Road,
their echoes morph into something softer—
the warm throb of a whāriki unrolling,
stitched from streetlight prayers.

I take a breath—
provincial mud to urban neon—
the hymn rewrites itself.

Legends made at Sinners.
Massive Attack at Staircase.
Ecstasy and revelations.
Rides on late-night yellow buses.

Plastic cups clink like Sunday's chalice,
voices braid like smoke,
and the lad I hardly know

feels the swell of unnamed belonging,
a constellation forming
among strangers in the dark.

No need to shout or take a stand—
it was a quiet revolution,
a ballet of shadows,
where shame slips off,
and kinship blooms
in half-lit alleys—
where Hape's call still carries.

I fold into the rhythm,
older than the game itself—
a hymn sung in black cotton,
pride, and mud,
a poetry written by bodies
finding kāinga on a road,
not knowing they'd never return.

—TOPHER SHIELDS (he/him)

Guada Mabuya

even the savages can recite all of the gospels.
confining constitutions to coffins of concrete

and I can only claw at what was once promised,
excavating the burial grounds of a lost memory

that might have belonged to you: a crane's wing
ensnared across the barbed wire. rainfall softens

to allow the displaced to set up their encampments
beneath the cemetery's statues—a final reminder

that we can still drown in the baptismal font, still
find our names written across the fangs of verses

that we once recited together during the bonfires.
a scorched telegram of an abandoned geography

left unreceived at the desk of an emptied handgun:
do you understand why the statues started walking?

do you understand why the texts no longer matter?
count all of the bodies hanging from the flagpoles.

form your hypothesis on the meaning of freedom.
I sit here in the aftermath of what I knew was me.

of what I *thought* was me. a body: a collection
of corpses. our bread has yet to fall from the sky.

the strings of the marionette are soaked in ink.
the only time we write is once the body breaks,

folds, realigns itself into recognizable symbols
capable of being reprinted, read at the eulogies,

rehearsed, finally recited by the representatives
only after the world begins to suspect savagery:

the barbed wire is to shelter us from invasions,
the amalgamation of mangled wings a reminder

that the devil can deceive us with the beautiful.
we simply halted the spread of the wicked wind.

the poets and novelists willingly stopped writing.
the bread? due to fall from the sky any time now.

and here we still sit in the aftermath of ourselves
being lulled to sleep by the serenades of strings

snapping in succession, speaking soliloquies
to the statues above us. the silent stone saints

who bear the weight of yet another generation.
perhaps they too are searching for their bodies.

perhaps they too imagined building homes.
but even the spirits among us have their curfews.

they stand beyond the rows of barbed wire, waiting
for us to remember the verses lost within the bonfire.

these unmarked headstones are the sprouting teeth
of a beast I was once promised was here to protect

us, the children of the displaced. the concrete coffins
remind me of a time where words constructed worlds

and the sunset was never feared. to return to that body.
to return to the original text of a long-forgotten gospel.

—JULIO CÉSAR VILLEGAS (he/him)

I ENLIST MY FRIEND IN THE ARRIVAL COMMITTEE

Assess: I ask him what we should prepare—food, drinks, entertainment, fun facts? He says all we need to bring is an atlas mind, everything else can wait. Maybe some convo is needed first, he says. He offers to make a gentle alien playlist, to make them feel more comfortable. We don't want to be parodying, so other than zoopzapzipshwap, what sounds might we fit in there?

Distract: I suggest we add the barred owl call that we all agree sounds like who cooks for you, who cooks for you all? I heard him this weekend, I tell my friend. I didn't dare get up and look outside, there were wasp nests nesting and I didn't want to be an intruder. Anyway, wasp sounds are less friendly than grandpa-owl asking about my cooking habits. What a thing. To be respectful of something only because it can hurt me. Anyway. Who cooks for you, alien? What is your food? What are your sounds? Assembled in the universe, do you know gestures? I lift my hand to gently, friendly-ly offer a hand sign, something moving, but not so fast it looks like a target. Or an attacker. I am careful to make you feel safe and welcome.

Negotiate: Not too welcome, I don't want you to think this is all yours, we still need some, okay most of it. Restate. There's a little plot with not much around it, 347814317857 miles away from us, that I guess you could have if you insist, but since we're lending it to you, you don't really have-have it in the way that you can keep it or pass it along to your future alienbebes. Restate. You can just be there for now. stationed, protecting it, keeping it running. I'll tell you what—why don't you set up a farm? a factory? What are your talents? It doesn't matter, a lesson can be taught to anyone desperate enough to want to be here.

—SHIVANI GUPTA (she/her)

desolation in the field

the body knocked out. and i'm trying to find a sorry for how desolation got stuck in the field. how the knock out projected and the body desolated, life wrenching off the bones she inherited from me. and i'm sorry this was the lifetime of pile ups. catastrophe after catastrophe ransacking under skin. unattended mother woundings and father woundings depressing calamity from a distance. and listen, i'm combing the field as fast as i can, begging vibration to tend to trauma's record and ruptures, but the body isn't tuning itself back and this curse isn't lifting off these bones. all i keep finding are places where the soul chipped too far off from the center, pockets where our childhood molded, where lineage held tight with grief. and i'm sorry your vessel held most potential for collapse, and fight and danger adhered to the esophagus, and white blood cells latticed preservation at the neck—throat an epic of a girl's crusade. and i'm trying to tell her i'm sorry the body became the thing to be sorry for, sorry the heart emptied out, sorry the meaning emptied out, sorry you're holding your body like you want it to end like it *is* an end, sorry, sorry, sorry life keeps thinning, slipping, knocking out of fucking orbit and now this course is speeding too fast toward a desolate plane and please, *please* i want to tell her the smallest details can lead back to a girl to find them and hook wrist onto the gridlines, it's almost over, its almost over

—VANESSA PEDROZA (she/her)

Mrs. Greystone

Mrs. Greystone's knocking at my door again.
She's keeping me up at night.
It all started back in October
when I saw her in the bathroom at the bar.
We locked eyes and I darted; she followed me back
into the party.
I ignored her, but she didn't stop trying,
vying for my attention.

The next morning she came to my door,
tapped on it with her long pinky nail.
"Don't you miss me, sweetie?"
she asks, saccharine-sweet, high fructose syrup.
She is thick and heavenly and divine.
"Don't you miss your dear friend, honey?"
I pull my blinds shut and I go back to bed.

I ran into Mrs. Greystone again at the party.
She was kissing my friend in the corner so sweetly,
her powder falling flush onto my friend's cheeks.
They beam, Mrs. Greystone moans.
They introduce me and I pretend I do not know her—
Mrs. Greystone, my dear old friend.

The next morning she came to my door,
knocked on it with a heavy fist.
"Why won't you speak to me, sweetie?"
she wails, sickeningly sour, post-nasal drip.
She is desperate and anxious and distressed.
"Don't you want your dear friend, honey?"
I make sure the deadbolt is locked and I go back to bed.

The next time I see Mrs. Greystone I am looking for her.
I was at a party and I imagined the way I used to feel
when she would kiss me, and I called her
and made the mistake of telling her I missed her.
I hear her chuckle and laugh and scream—
our long anticipated reunion, at last.

I go back to my place and an hour later she arrives and is waiting.
She is slamming her body against my door.
"Open the fuck up, sweetie!"
she demands, she is sick and twisted and evil.
"Don't you realize you need me, honey?
Don't you realize it's always been me, honey?
Who do you think got you through those dark times, cutie?
Why do you think you had so much fun in college, baby?
Remember High Falls mid-November? That was all me, sugar!
You think you are so confident, darling?
All those friends you used to have?
They were all because of me, honey!
Where are they now, sweetheart?
Not with you, are they?
Where am I, honey?
I have always stayed!"

Mrs. Greystone is knocking my door off of its hinges.
I scream as she bursts into my home,
the home I have created to protect myself from those like her.
I tell her to get out, but it is too late.
She is on top of me, my head in her hands,
my lips slack, hers pursed.
She leans towards my face, it's not so bad,
my dear old friend, the smell of her perfume gets me excited.
She can feel it; she grinds her hips; I arch away
because this close I feel all of her:
her crooked nose, her yellow teeth,
her greasy hair, her sunken cheeks,
her undereyes, her nasty breath.
So I pinch my nose and look away.
She tries again.
I do not stray.
You tried your best, Mrs. Greystone, honey,
but you lost again today.

—Satori (she/her)

A scent like church in here
Torn cuticles and no underwear—my Tuesday

My past: exacto knife, finely trimmed letters
        How random it all became:

An undoing. An upset. A disaster.

There is a typewriter here.
            Floating shift.

An undoing. An upset. A disaster
        with no autocorrect

Art Date (with Adam) on display
The sharing of space

The text wasn't clear, so I could get drunk.

An open suitcase.
A window.
The street.
I can't reach any of it in the time I have left.

Film strip.
Eye flower.
Yarn on the wall.
The fan turns.

A poster:
"Bridal Excellence" (I am not.)
I've forgotten how.

Sometimes poems are given as gifts:
"ripple, glue, dye" (life motto)

Industrial sink.
Beer in the fridge.
A clean toilet.
Dried mango.
White onions.
Pitted dates.

Something is taking shape:
unknown categories, swollen rivers.

The thread is lost or smothered in pins—
my mother's sewing box.

—JENNY BEMJAMIN (she/her)

Chocolate salami, porcelain bowl, beaten eggs, scraping nails against a metal bowl, their bodies once combined when I wasn't looking. They transfer chocolate mixture into plastic wrap meant for frosting, no one corrects them, no one judges when they leave the fridge open for hours, the worst of the food spoiling, the best of the food wilting. *You only put your honesty in one part of your poem,* he said to me, so therefore he goes in the poem. I want to use the cream cheese knife. I want to use any knife. It has been seventeen days. It's a Sunday and my heart is marching out of my chest. I watch her coax him to make my father's difficult pie crust. *She has a terrible relationship with her father,* I can hear the woman saying. Oh, my dear, his shape looms in the doorway and I wonder about the nature of violence. What if the nightmares I've had for weeks turn out to be true? Never you mind. Next come guests. They bring pints of blackberries, raspberries, rainbow berries, and lies. The worst of my mood will arrive when I am alone in the private part of the house, at the lip of the tub, wondering about the water and the weapons. I used to think I was so clear when I used words like *blood* and *paste* and *hate* and *haste* but when I brought up the activity, you claimed you'd never heard of it before. Is this, too, a lie? I can hear her voice, honeyed, dripping through the vents. Her compliments to you are dripping across the walls, spilling onto my head. She smells like cantaloupes. She eats overripe fruits without gagging. She snips grape stems and stacks their bodies into elk horns. Even still, after all that dizzyingly easy conversation, you turned to me. I wonder if you look because you can't remember what my face looks like. Or are you wondering. Enough with the Manchego. Please fill the scabs on my wrists with mint sprigs. Melt my mouth. Break spice to my throat. I didn't think I still cared, but here we are. When she asks to add my hands to the pie, I oblige. She watches us, eating a large pomegranate, chunks falling all over her blouse. Maybe I never mattered. Marinated rosemary, blueberry hearts, tomato clusters, cut vines, blood oranges, verbal digs, sprigs, nuts, I love you and then I don't, onion powder, my mood is sour, drained apples, mushy oil, sour pepper, and more.

—**Sam Moe** (she/her)

DIFFERENT STATES

New bones settle, limbs stretching
in the slow agony of seasons.
So many years, a crystalline instant
we forget the moment it washes over us.
Longing, and the physicality of it—
desperately resurrecting ourselves
at every sun-dappled lawn. Familiar-wrong
children with charcoal smoke hair,
chlorine sticky skin.

(The mosaic of ourselves
as we exist in memory—
always doing everything wrong.)

I think of the baby teeth I pressed
my tongue to, once, learning myself
by a stranger's name. How it felt to see
each one liberated in a quick-snap
instant of sweet-bitter blood.

(How an absence
is a presence, too.)

I imagine them still carefully
tucked away in the soapstone box
on your dresser, and miss you
with a psychosomatic pang of
loss in my jaw.

Every day an effigy, thinking
that happiness exists solely in the form
of what we were—what we can never
return to. Yet it is through becoming
that you turn around and see:
the cage was always just a cage.

We are not solidly joined and inextricable.
Reassemble the pieces,
the beginning place is here.

The path forward is
patient and inevitable.

—Sylvia Goreaux (they/them)

YOU ARE HERE

This love affair is a garden in disguise.
Let me explain:

A peach bleeding juice on a chapel step,
by a white veil sailing on the wire fence.

Old gods hunger, something pulpy rots
in the sun, as an ache and declaration.

It's your choice. What grows there,
what dies there, and who tends it?

We take turns building inside a soft space.

—STEPHANIE VALENTE (she/her)

WHAT IS IT LIKE TO BE A CAT?

> *In so far as I can imagine this (which is not very far),*
> *it tells me only what it would be like for* me
> *to behave as a bat behaves. But that is not the question.*
> *I want to know what it is like for a* bat *to be a bat.*
>
> —Thomas Nagel, "What Is It Like To Be a Bat?"

I. I listened to the vet consider the best course of action
for our elderly cat.
She said we could elect to have their trained surgeons
examine her nose
but she might not survive the operation, the vet warned us
of asserting liability,
nor can we treat nasal cancer.

Nasal cancer is a death sentence for a cat, she didn't say,
careful not to destroy the illusion of animal science and care.

But trust the science:

> *You might be confronted with the knowledge of knowing*
> *she has nasal cancer.*

II. The vet first used
the language of the scientist,
those words largely technical,
a recitation from previous appointments.
When her tone moved to uncertainty,
she relied less on the objective and
extrapolated her subjectivities onto the situation.
She probably thought she was being humane
when she kept referring to one of her house cats
who was also ill and required commitment to care:

> *It would make me feel better if I really knew,*
> *what was causing her discomfort,*
> *what was causing her pain.*

III.   Nagel begins by charging that philosophers, like scientists,
                are reductionists
                that they too
                "share the general human weakness for explanations
                of what is incomprehensible in terms suited for what is
                familiar
                and well understood, though entirely different."

        Any subjective experience is connected with a single point of
        view, thus
        destroying any objective mind-body-consciousness dilemma.

        The experience of bats, then, can only be expressed in
        speculative analogies from a
        human's perspective.

        What a human thinks it is like to be a bat.

IV.   Being caring
        and
        being careful
        are not always
        synonymous acts.

V.   I once gave a talk at a university workshop and
        cited a line from *Transcendent Kingdom*, a novel about
        a neuroscientist's experiment on mice:
        ". . . the truth is we don't know what we don't know."

VI.   Four months after her in/formal diagnosis, the tumor grew—
        some days, it looked less oppressively invasive,
        other days, it threatened to eclipse her left green eye.

        We knew her illness was terminal
        when she sneezed blood,
        her tiny body trembled as she held her breath,

she would look from one person to the next,
and all we could say to her was
       there, there
       it's okay, it's okay,
when we knew we weren't being honest to her,
nor to ourselves.

VII.   On the many sleepless nights, unfair human-animal
analogies
comparisons
 haunt my mind.
Our cat couldn't describe her pain to us,
neither could my father at the end of his life,
 his whispers gradually disappeared
 and only air came out,
both had trouble breathing,
both had trouble eating,
my father couldn't swallow food,
his heart was weak, his lungs were drowning,
our cat could no longer see her food,
so I had to turn her bowl strategically
so she could eat,
but she had trouble keeping her food down,
both woke me up during early mornings
because their pain prevented them from resting.

VIII.   At 10 in the evening, we drove to the emergency animal clinic,
where we sat in the waiting room for an hour
before a technician came to us to conduct triage.
They listened to her heart rate, examined her ears
and concluded she was not high-risk.
        Had they asked me, I'd have tried to recall the image of
        our cat,
        mouth open, unable to breathe,
        eyes rolled up to her head,
        ears downcast.

My partner once told me we'd know it was time when it
was time.

Almost an hour later, the vet examined her thoroughly in a
private room
where they said her ribs were distended, bulging out,
perhaps because she was struggling to breathe,
and they would recommend putting her to sleep
as it would be absolutely warranted.
Though the wording was vaguely legal,
the vet avoided absolute language,
everything was
a recommendation,
a hypothetical,
a conditional.

—ANNA NGUYEN (she/her)

RITUAL

I had to remake what was unmade:
petals lifted to a winter tree,
slipped into empty stem gums.
Unfurled orange
absent fruit, a lingering scent:
this exact sweetness must return.

—JULIETTA BEKKER (she/they)

*First published by *orangepeel*

HOW THE MOUNTAIN EARNED ITS BONES

Virginia,
Vesuvius, Virginia
at the foot of a mountain so old,
        that it had no bones inside

stooped over
by the wind and the rain

                covered
in creeks and cricks

the weight
of all the air of the world

                coming down,
on top of it

There abouts, is a careful house—
white and stone, with a water wheel
winding, whining

And when she sits outside it at night—
she sees a thousand of her
own eyes out there, in the trees
peeping, blinking   So

she looks up
way, way up
away instead

To see the rosy moon
returning
recounting the setting sun

they said

Burn, burn
don't   turn   around

burn, burn
sky to ground
run, run
don't look away
burn it down
if you can't stay

But she had to
stay, or they'd follow
her out and down, off the mountain—in
want of bone

So she stayed and looked and sang and burned
and the mountain kept the 103,206 bones it earned, that smoke had left
                    where she stayed,
          & yet
              & yet
          in ashen grave

—BIANCA AMBROSINO (she/her)

34

GENEALOGY

Family. An appliance
like a kitchen sink, furnace, oven, refrigerator.

Comes with a name, a thing of syllables umbilically.
grafted onto a being. Recorded, remembered, washed,

gifted, afflicted, infected, as history vomits you up each day.

—MARK FLECKENSTEIN (he/him)

THE CITY CAN'T SAVE YOU

You tried to put me in a city and it almost killed me
Neon lights and dancing girls
I'd drag you along to go stargazing and you'd leave the headlights on
Little not-quite-country not-quite-girl
I gave up asking for camping trips once I stopped running outside in barefeet
Your lights were fun until they weren't
Then I was burning fuses to keep you happy
If you wouldn't see my stars, maybe I could see yours
I was moon blind until I came to as a
          party girl city girl
Being held while surrounded by the scent of sex you had with someone else
You taught me to cherish being alone
I suppose I taught you that too
In truth, I am scared to go home
What if the lakebed doesn't remember the shape of my toes?

—CRYPTID PARKE (they/them)

IF I WERE FRANKENSTEIN'S MONSTER

The new age one, immortal,
unlike the 1800s where death
was all around.

I doubt I'd stand in the Arctic
or pause to stare at the sun
if death was not an option

I would try hibernation
for a season, let this world churn
itself a new shade.

There is a story I was told
growing up, about gods and demons
being partners in crime

to churn the ocean, a mountain
as the churning rod
& serpent as the rope

when the good and bad unite
there must be a reason & reason
there was: immortality

drunk on Amrit
someone had to drink
the counter-measure poison

come Shiva,
my namesake
or I his?

bring Prithvi, bring Apas,
bring Agni, bring Vayu,
bring Akaash—

come Shiva, let's plot a reset.
Blue-throated,
he's called destructor

& savior, but is also the one to chop
his son's head off & replace
it with the nearest elephant,

so I guess we can't surrender
just yet. Not give up all our riches
to a temple or a god,

not trust in the press
of a sold paper
& the godemons on the news,

not love when there
is loss of self
guaranteed,

not pluck flowers
that were meant for
someone else,

but who I am to know
where to best spend
what you have when

time is a measure of passing
love, a promise of longing
inheritance, assured disappointment

God.
How do the bears sleep
with so much happening outside?

—SHIVANI GUPTA (she/her)

on air plants, in the panamanian cloud forest

there are hemiepiphytes, says the british expat, who starts rooted
then it's not an epiphyte at all, is it?

starts and stays are very different verbs, i realize
i think the hemiepiphytes know a little bit about
my language

two – primary hemiepiphytes

there are hemiepiphytes who *absorb water from the atmosphere*, says the
british expat
to absorb water from the atmosphere would be every kid who
takes all their love from the world around them
instead of from the ground that should have raised them up

they make their own cup to drink from says the british expat
this solves some problems but creates others
because in order to obtain water they must retain water
you keep from quenching your thirst so that you don't thirst later

but when it works
the soil they create is much richer than the soil on the ground
and the host-tree might take offense, creating aerial roots to steal the
nutrients
that the plant worked so hard to make

and if i understand it right, the plants are always trying to grow down,
to reach the ground and settle, but those aerial roots chase them up,
jealousy of success despite the odds, leaving them stuck in the climb
skyward, until there's nothing left but the sun and shrivelling

three – true epiphytes

why suggests purpose and i have no idea what the purposes of these are,
says the british expat, who now lives happily in panamá

he's talking now about true epiphytes
they have no roots in the ground, ever
no need to grow up or down

they're parasitic, michael tells us—that's his name
trees shed them, he says, because of competition for nutrients
what must it take to thrive, your home always trying to shake you off?

but, true epiphytes are resilient, *adaptable*
it's easy to dry out when you're always so close to the sun
but fight back enough
and you learn to retain water.

—EMELIA DELAPORTE (she/her)

*First published by *Nova Literary-Arts Magazine*

HOLY ANOREXIC (KAREN CARPENTER AS DREAM GIRL) (PATRON SAINT OF RIB CAGES)
(TUFTS OF HAIR FALLING OUT) (I MADE IT ALL THE WAY TO CONFIRMATION AND ALL I
GOT IS THIS CATHOLIC GUILT)

I am told I am holy
by the Wiki page last
edited six days ago.

I feel a cause deep
in my gut but when
I ask Chat GPT for
advice I get sent to
a hotline and probably
kill 100 trees.

When Catherine did
this she was canonized,
curse my luck I am sick
when I should be a god.

I am not a religious person
except for Colosseums
and a forty day fast.
*Your very being
is a miracle,*
according to my mom.

She is all good sauce with
the immersion blender and
I am caught up on the canon,

I want to be the canon.

(goodbye karen, goodbye singing, goodbye religion, goodbye tomato soup)

—NIAMH CAHILL (she/her)

You are a miniature deer swimming in a bowl of mother's best soup. *Wellness* is not a word in your vocabulary. You returned home earlier with a warning and your partner said at least your fingers weren't bad. He doesn't understand the pathways, rivers, vengeance. Earlier, you told the wrong person the right story about the blood, twisted. You wanted to say *burnout,* but language tripped into *birds, burners, blatant, blessings.* There is a bagel shop down the block from your late abuelita's apartment. When you were younger, your mother and her sister would stand in line with miniature orange juices and enough cash to get everyone bagels with more than three toppings. The other day, someone asked why you were afraid everyone would leave. He asked if people had done that before. How to explain the first to abandon you were family. When you return to the bagel shop as an adult, no one accompanies you. Your family thinks you're bad news. Would it even matter, if you told the truth to these people? Keep swimming in the red soup. Dodge the mushy carrots. Use the potato wedges as life rafts. Become exhausted talking about sickness and illness. No one believes your pain. Outside, tornado season strips lawns and roofs. One of your friends has her house intact yet three garage lights have been plucked clean off their metal spires. Someone makes a joke. You hide in the closet and eat pizza like your life depends on it. One of your friends says you have terrible eating habits. Tell him again about the eating disorder. Tell him to stop pretending with the stapler and the box cutter and the windows, but he already knows. Are you listening? This story has been told. This soup lacks a proper flavor profile. The bowl gives a concussion. Your skin is aware. Your blood is the mood of others. You could try to explain the flashbacks, how your face molded after the blow, how you know nicknames and street names and the stamping of gold code. Give the knowledge away. Let your personality be devoured. Listen: it doesn't rain here; it never did.

—SAM MOE (she/her)

throw away the house if the clock stops

I tried to throw it
away in my mind;

remember that little
yellow house isn't yellow

or mine anymore, but
I don't believe people,

things, places are
disposable. I don't

want to un-build a
house. I want to

remember what we
had there, hold it

in my heart like a
red door, like oak trees.

I saw us there in
a dream, lemonade

and beer on the deck
in bright open summer

evenings pulled forth
through layers of

dust like excavation.
I am an archeologist

of memory and I am
bad at my job,

always crying over
spilt artifacts,

always stuck in
remembering golden

times. I'm sure in
retrospect they weren't

even gold, but yellow.
feeding myself paint

chip breakfasts and
old dog afternoons,

I feast on memory but
never get full.

—ROWAN ELLIOT GIBSON (they/them)

THE SINGULAR THREAD

Intimacy, labor, how many years ago?

You began to knit your own underwear

Onto yourself. How each of these days

Elides before the eyes into a distant land

Only drawing near as an incense

That fades into the rusted teal of a penny.

Out of this veil of oxidation, an orb-weaver

Fingers forth, spits a hundred needles,

And spins the singular thread.

—ANDREW RADER HANSON (he/him)

SEASIDE EULOGY

Summer laps at the shore
of September, refusing to let up,
but the tide keeps pulling
it farther and farther.

Crass yellow folds
into an amber glow, like embers
of a dying fire, turning to ashes
in my mouth.

Swirling oil through water,
I forget what I look like.
My origami face, a smile
one moment, a crane the next.

I let the dusky ramen broth
of the sea unclog
my heartpores, gulp
saltwater to cleanse my tongue.

But the crystal ball moon knows
my marsupial sadness
that splinters like a chicken bone
in my throat, and

it can sense a storm
is brewing. I reach
to unzip the horizon
and let it out.

—ELLA B. WINTERS (she/they)

WHAT THE ORACLE GAVE ME

A dead canary in a velvet pouch
One nearly empty perfume bottle labeled *Choose*
One cufflink from a man I never met
A mirror that only reflects my future
A letter with no return address

—STEPHANIE VALENTE (she/her)

three piece harmony

before it began, I went to the table blindfolded and felt my way through.
calcified, textured crisp. hot, curving grips. wet, like sinking. a pitch cry as I
pushed over a slosh, the sound spreading wild. something was exotic in
the way we grasped, gothic in the unknowing. you slipped finger after
finger against the bare of my shoulders and took me to my seat. then
disappeared into the dark.

I sat for years, statuesque. pulled the mask off eventually to see what was
left. there it all unfolded, the burnt flesh made fuzzy again with fungus, the
exposed and hollowed home-grown bones, the sideways cake with
submerged berries. running the length of the table was the liquor I had
spilled, gleaming amber against lucid silver trays. at the end was you.

the house lights came up when I realized, and you were found crucified to
your own chair at the head of the table. time had come for you like it comes
for all of us. melted the skin from your eyelids to settle in the socket
hollows. cracked the jaw and left it hanging. splintered wrinkles. I reset the
chalice before me, watched it fill with your old blood.

—MIKAYLA ELIAS (they/them)

Help Needed

Picking berries on my plot
has become a full-time job.
Here I am, the victim
of my own success,
hand perilously plunging
into the barbed thicket
to pluck at scarlet morsels,
competing with the slugs
for sustenance,
the bees complaining
at being disturbed
on their daily rounds.
The thorns, sharp
as tongues, feast
on my arms, until I can't
tell where the berry
juice begins and mine
ends.

My limbs grow
long and slender, soft
hairs bristle into
needles, small flowers break
free from my fingers.
I am verdant and lush.
The bees flock to suck
on my nectar, I let slugs glide
up my branches, softly
nibble on the plump, red
flesh. But then, there is
nothing I can do,
rooted and voiceless
as I am, to save
myself when a hand
reaches in to pluck
a berry.

—ELLA B. WINTERS (she/they)

Poem about Love

Well. I remember
drunk-high-won't come-down
you were there
and I said Can, sorry,
May we live forever
and you looked straight up
like the Disaronno
I tried   to   chase
that chased us   right back
But my God, we lived it, and got
the better
I screamed more and threw up;
bid adieu in my escape to the
pisser, where I ought to rest

And the morning after your grace,
I was still alive
divinely baptized
in chunks of last night
and before, and before, and before
again, and again, and again

—Zac Gosney (he/they)

SAFE PLACE WITH NETTLES

If I speak of the woods, I mean the place you go when he comes at night, fingers moulding the clay of your throat, mouth spitting anger into your sleep as you crush your eyes shut, imagining yourself stretched out in a wild green space, its easy silence like sitting with a friend. Now you're a child again, crushing dandelions (you call them piss-a-beds) on your arm, swatching yourself fancy with fake tan, their sharp stink like peeing in roadside crab grass, mum waiting patiently for you, dad tapping his watch, the dash. Nettles tower around you in your safe place, their spines white hairs on tanned bare summer arms. Grasp them—tall electric eels—to feel something different from love-hating this man who's slowly killing you. He's hardly here, now you're in the nettles. He's not on top and you can't smell his beer-breath, hear his heavy silence. You're sinking soft and downwards inside that cool, dark place that held you as a child. It's crayoning your whole world green.

—KATE HORSLEY (she/her)

A Gay Roué With Stars

Your lazy figure loafs
across the green, wrapped, I see
from here, in suede
to sing the moving music
of your steps
and cinched
with a chain
of flickering pentacles meant
to cast such a deep, mysterious spell. Stargazing, unaware
of me, you casually drop a rose. You're finished
with that petty plaything now.

Dark-haired, dark-eyed dark soul, don't stroll near. The message
of your wistful gaze
is none compared
to mine. No deep book could possibly comprehend.

—Ken Anderson (he/him)

I'M FINE!

restlessness rustles, a ruthless truth
too thorny, a toothy swarming mess.
better plaster it faster, smooth over,
leave no gaps or cracks.
but the humming thrum is patient,
you are young,
it will be back.

—ROWAN ELLIOT GIBSON (they/them)

Vivisectioning a Love Poem

As the last real romantic, a cynic in a ragged, out of fashion suit,
holes in my shoes, and the whiff of respiratory despair,
I'm yours. Completely.
Don't be alarmed or find it necessary for an excuse
(however polite and faultlessly construed)
to rewind the tape and be elsewhere.
There is no there or here or time. Once,
yes. A smidgen.
With just enough edge to snare a piece of wind,
an amazed howl, suggesting human emotions
come in different colors and temperatures
and depend on music stained in the background.
And because it's nearly love or next available compromised emotion
clipped savaged flayed and oh so perfect!
A blood cry, blood free of veinous constraint, the heart's attitude and pushy
ill-mannered demands about where to be when.
Finally, finally giving *why* its true color.

—MARK FLECKENSTEIN (he/him)

in the moment of loss (eulogy for the thunder)

she described the birth as a flash arc event. the tearing a visible kinetic,
kicking and screaming. it was a demonstration of the crash of potential—
paced, then tired, then urgent. the veil vanished, trapping her in the face of
this wild. and oh, how she changed the glory of permanence. the thunder
touched her and left scars. we are all in need of the rain, the purity of
collapsing into our original fragments. understand the thunder, its
compression into diamond chords.

—MIKAYLA ELIAS (they/them)

// BLOOD MOON //

the blood is back
the blood your womb gives you
when you don't give it much but
the tease of a fucking from
an inanimate silicone cock

oh I remember
you think to yourself
being a woman &
all the things that come with that
even those you do not ask for

it's the first period you've had since
you first had nurses inject
hormones into your asscheek
every twelve or however
many weeks

it's also a full moon in pisces
how fitting—you're a pisces & full
moons are for letting go of
things that no longer serve you
at least that's what the internet told you

you are letting go of things that no longer serve you
like the womb lining you hope won't ever wax gibbous
like when you kept your body in an induced
coma of infertility
& didn't comprehend how it made you numb

you are so horny these days but not for love
no no you're horny for love but you can't have it
no no you have it the love but you can't say it
you have the love but not the sex
you have the sex if silicone counts

the first thing you think when you
see the red on your panties after remembering is

how am I going to masturbate
the lube stains line your silk nightdress like ghosts &
ghosts are not creatures who bleed

—DEVON WEBB (she/her)

ENTERRADOS

It wounds wonderful.
Why settle for a captive audience when I could have a hostage one?
Listen to this or I'll kill myself.

Lick my glitteris.
Masticate my microplastics.
We're burying ourselves in our own plastic coffins.
Rose colored wreckage.
Unrottable.

You're a forever chemical.
You won't stay dead.

—MOLLY ROSE STRUGATZ (she/her)

I Count 7 Fish at the Dentist Office's Tank, My Teeth Bleed 1 Minute In

The kind technician tells me that I need to wear my mouth guard more while idyllic Europe scenes from YouTube play on the large scene in front. When they get to the country my most recent heartbreak is from, I spit into the basin, bright red and foamy. She tells me that the key to life is flossing morning and night, I am trying so hard not to bite her fist in my jaw that my eyes start to water. When my Dad was sick everything felt neon. The walls of my high school, the river I spent my afternoons on, instead of grey I felt hyperaware. This is the school I could graduate from without my Dad in the audience, the tallest one there. This is the race I will probably lose, no one to dissect each mistake with after. They ran out of veins to poke in my Dad and brought in the experts, a tiny old woman with a knack for blood work. When I heard he was sick I went to school and home three times until it caught me on the purple carpet of my old bedroom. The technician scrapes my teeth, telling me I need to have a softer hand when I brush, and I try to feel grounded in what I can see in the room. Pictures of the Jurassic Coast flash on the screen, a photo of the technician and a little boy who could be her son on a ledge, a beautiful model on the cover of a tooth whitening campaign. Lorraine, the technician, makes small talk while I bleed, telling me she moved her daughter into her NYU dorm this Saturday. Because her hand is in my mouth I can't tell her that when I moved in four years ago I had practiced saying goodbye to my Dad so many times in a waiting room that Ohio didn't hurt as bad. She says that both her and her daughter cried and instead I blink twice, trying to tell her that I understand.

—NIAMH CAHILL (she/her)

AMNIOTIC INHERITANCE

Before my birth carved the world
into separate things, I floated
in the boundary between
self and not-self, warm brine
tasting of salt and iron and something
faintly sweet I'd later know
as the flavor of new skin,
vernix and the particular myrrh
of new life.

These fluids carried secrets
older than memory,
narratives of grandmothers
who survived by staying mute,
their unspoken truths metabolizing
into my growing bones.

In that liquid darkness,
absence became presence.
Every sound (heartbeat, bloodrush,
the distant drum of my mother's voice)
was also my own.

§

Thumb to mouth,
I rehearsed self-soothing in waters
where cortisol storms
passed through permeable membranes,
training my forming nervous system
in the frequency of vigilance,
and the wavelength of waiting
for danger to pass.

§

The water that held me
held my ancestors' fear,

hormones bitter as bile,
generations of women
swallowing words until silence
accumulated like plaque in arteries,
until it thickened into poison.

My mother's stress
taught my cells before I had ears,
before I had choice,
my nascent heart attuning to
the cadence of wariness,
her body's stories
merging with the ones my cells
had begun writing,
preparing to carry forward.

§

Then came the breaking:
walls contracting, pressure mounting,
water draining from the only world I knew.
The tunnel narrowed, crushed,
pushed me from salt to air,
from spirit into flesh.
That first breath tore through me,
sharp and cold and utterly alone,
my lungs learning to pull
what the cord had carried,
the ocean somewhere else,
outside of me.

And yet the hands that caught me
were made of the same water,
the air that filled my lungs
held the memory of the cosmic sea.

What spilled in my breaking
was darker than water—

meconium, my body's first oracle,
staining cloth as tea leaves
steep and tell,
patterns swirling on cotton and sand
as though the universe
could not wait to reveal
what my grandmothers already knew:
we are born with our fortunes
already written inside us,
the sediment of ancient tides
we will spend our lives
learning to read.

§

The water revealed all to us,
showed me, you, and everybody:
boundaries were semipermeable,
not walls. We discovered separation
long after we'd forgotten
we began as one body of water
when we struggled to breathe
in our mothers' tide.

We forgot that struggle
was not leaving the water
but teaching ourselves to carry it

inside our lungs,
our veins, our tears,

revealing we are never
only ourselves
but also everyone
who came before,
their fears and courage both
dissolved in the same
amniotic sea
still pulsing in the rhythm
of our blood, our mothers'
pulse,
the first drum
we ever knew.

Even now, in air,
in this world divided
into separate things,
I taste salt when I cry,
feel the tide pull
in the marrow of my bones,
and cannot tell
where the ocean ends
and I begin—
perhaps we never
were apart.

—ASHLEY PARKER OWENS (she/her)

Maybe we're alike, you and me. Maybe something happened to change your relationship to men. To women. To anyone. Nearby is a barista with a hose, washing the sidewalk. Everything reminds me of New York City, which is to say, everything reminds me of my late grandmother and the parrot down the street who flew to Queens after someone left his cage open, so maybe this is about loss. Pumpkin spice and the fire hydrants are clear water flares where I used to play as a child. Going home feels like an emergency. Lately my therapist has been trying to get me to name grief. She told me I can borrow her hope if I need to. I try to work every fact about myself into a conversation because I don't know if we'll ever see each other again. Which is another way of saying if you hate me, I'll disappear. Cinnamon in my coffee and monarchs in autumn, I wanted to relapse but I'm trying to garden instead. Vanilla scones and the beds I have to sleep in where I've been raped. Where my mother was molested. One foot out the door, Massachusetts is a dying ember in my mind. When will I become safe? When will men raising their voices cease to scare me. Do you still love me, or should I get a triple espresso shot? She has a bumper sticker on her car that has words like *bestie* and *Capricorn*. Darling, I'm going under. A man I once thought I loved left me during summer before turning into a ram. He now lives inside a drum. This, too, is a fairytale.

—SAM MOE (she/her)

We fossils.
We tectonic plates
shifting in the night.
Our bodies,
our lubricated joints
bathed in ocean-sweat.
And
my mouth
your acoustic lobe
living decades apart.

—CASSADY O'REILLY HAHN (he/him)

If distance had a temperature.
It would range from warm to cold. Weight padded
From the rolling minutes. To hours. To days.
Blink once and a week passes by.
Blink twice, then a whole year.
I see the moonlight and thank the heavens
For this bit of warmth. Silver lining of the night,
Sadness follows as it grows old and disappears.
Until the new one emerges.
Weigh heavy on me, like a blanket.
I travel the distance as the wind rises,
Hoping to reach the fleeing light to the new day.
Gauge the temperature carefully
With each step you take. Know what you can handle.
Or find out early, well before you begin your journey.
I still find myself looking over my shoulder
For the many turns I could've taken.
Decisiveness evades me, of this I wish I learned more.
A heart of uncertainty impacts the course of your actions,
And leaves you the burden of carrying the weight of regret.

—RICHARD A. QUIROZ (he/him)

Little hearts, cut out
of every page
    She had a book
full of holes—
    little missing heart
shapes

Piles of paper palpitations
in hardcover
        &
An empty wall,
suddenly studded with
every loose nail in the house

She hung a hundred lockets
there
&
in the center—
one broken pocket watch

Pick up the little hearts
Put them in the hanging
lockets

Wind the watch,
wind the watch

—BIANCA AMBROSINO (she/her)

VESSELS

Noah ignores a drowning Eve;
after all, the animals need space.
Her tears are lost in the rushing deluge.
Maybe there's room on the Flying Dutchman?

Cruise ships sail like floating petri dishes
loaded high with endless shrimp.
The front half of the Titanic and Andrea Gail
hold on to each other for dear life.

Pi and his Tiger drift somewhere offshore
trying to get the story straight.
Old man Santiago finally lands a giant marlin.
Will he row it back to shore uneaten?

The crew of the Nautilus suffers from the bends.
A Yellow Submarine implodes.
The Mayflower gives one look and turns around,
only to crash bow-first into the Santa Maria.

—MAXWELL BAUMAN M.F.A. (he/him)

65

Awake

I'm moth dust
        eyelids barely open
The dark sits out my window
        and I feel afraid
I fell asleep in a fire last night
                                thinking of him
Morning by lithium flashlight—
                                train tunnel to my bed
the fire now a ghost my mind made

The day will cog on
        I feel the unease of work

        the gratitude
of being   the alone
        a self in the folds

the crumbling house
                                overgrown yard
                        buried metals of a failed
                                                marriage
I wished for
        courage
        in an open field
                        of long grasses with fur caps
like dancers in fairy tales
                        they make soup from stones, cleave trees in two

If I fall back to sleep
        I wonder if
        I'd forget
        not this world
but the moments that separate space—
        the demarcations from the veins of my hands

                                        my mother's hands
weaving silence the stars
                        that hide wounds
we leave in dreams

                              —JENNY BEMJAMIN (she/her)

crashing into the earth through a narrow aisle

she imagines it: a leaking of spirit back
into the earth, love returned to the
dust we all once were. before it was
preserved in formaldehyde, this love
was the antidote to the rainy season.
now ice freezes against the briefcases
of soulless three-pieces and pantsuits,
wind brings it back north toward
home. the wound was open before
the bullet dropped into the chamber.
the case was shut before it could be
opened. the verdict was called before
it was read aloud. this love was found
guilty of

selfish empathy. this fate fell heavy on
the shoulders of a cursed kid with a
simple answer–no. *before you make
it, say yes to everything.* casket open,
she stands like family, like sentry. she
takes a picture before the closing
scene. she throws the first
handful of earth, feels relief. feels guilt.
she can talk her way out of anything,
except this mounting earth. she smells
the blood in the
air, crawls inside its stench.

—MIKAYLA ELIAS (they/them)

PILGRIMAGE

I never wanted a home
nor a *Lotus Sutra*
I am not a lotus eater

a home is a place
to hang history

floating
in etymological
soundfacts

a privilege
that is created

by language
illusions

—BRIAN L. JACOBS PHD. (he/they)

PATRON SAINTS

My best friend wasn't raised Catholic, but her boyfriend was. He tells her the stories he learned in church every Sunday and she imagines them the same way I imagine falling in love after I spend the night asking my Tarot cards about a woman who won't text me back tomorrow. She walks away with vague ideas of sacraments and confessionals, decides to believe in patron saints the way she believes in astrology.

She chooses a saint for herself, reads through stories on Britannica and sifts through them, each one more horrifying than the last, settles on Laura Vicuña because she was just a normal girl, because "she just really loved the church, and they decided that was enough".

That night, I Google the saint I chose for the first time in 20 years, searching for meaning I can claw out like a tumor. St. Lucy, Patron Saint of the Blind, plucked her own eyes out to make herself less desirable to a man who wanted her, a metaphor so obvious I'm not sure it's worth writing, and I wonder who my patron saint would be if I could choose over again, could shed the one I'd chosen at 12-years-old while my mother spent evenings weaving guilt into my veins.

Is there a patron saint of women trying to figure out who they are without their mother there to tell them? Of a woman finding desire for the first time in her 30s, wondering if it's too late to learn how to love, checking the weight of an orgasm in the palm of her hands and imagining what God would think of the want she fills between the cracks of every poem she writes. I imagine trailing my fingers across her throat, can almost feel her hands between my thighs, and it's holier than any God I could have imagined.

I know forgiveness is the virtue I'm meant to strive towards, remember teachers and priests evangelizing it, can line up all the times I've been told to forgive and have buried my resentment to make space for it as a timeline the length of my spine. But is there a patron saint of people who aren't inclined towards forgiveness, who can tell me where to put down all the anger I've been carrying since birth, since I inherited it from my mother and from her mother before her?

I'll spend forever reckoning with the impact of a God I never quite believed in on my life, will never really be able to make out the blurred line between *His* voice in my head and my mother's.

—KIERSTEN MCMONAGLE (she/her)

award's season (winter's wake)

the academy leers through the keyhole.
at their marks, they adjust their dilated lines of sight.
inside, there is a struggle under the light of a red omen.
we're live. the early angles are soft, illuminating the roundness:
swelling pupils, fingers, tongues, joints.
in hundreds of thousands of seconds, this is gone.
the tender moments erode. there is the fumble for organs
slumped by the cruelty of time. voices arch in white noise.
they score the scene. and soon, the sound is a kettle boiling over.
the subject of this composition is grappling for
a taste lost to the heat of time, lilted into nimbus.
the academy looks on at the exerted beads of sweat, salivates.
tonight, the rain will be the blood of their young,
and they will drink. the soiled bedsheets will be left
to stink and rot in a room of ghosts.
the subjects leave the shot, and the room is restaged.

—MIKAYLA ELIAS (they/them)

Oracular

Bird bones & tea leaves tell me nothing,
dreams leave no footprints to follow
in the morning.
I've outlived my ability to see the future.
What now? I'll augur nightfall
in the stain of sunsets,
rain in the shape of clouds,
death in a skeleton:
predictable mathematics.

—JULIETTA BEKKER (she/they)

BLACKOUT

While I swallow silence & seconds
        with bottom-shelf liquor
        pour over our plot at the kitchen sink

bathwater slow-crawls up the edge
of your tub   drowning out
        the impending crash   (and burn)

The bathroom door cracks open
        cold sliver of light meeting
                hardwood floor—

heart-wrenching how each needs the other.

The stillness outside breaks in half
        sends snow-covered tree branches crashing

into the wall with both hands.

I didn't know it was a sign at the time
        but, God forgive me—

I do now.

—NICHOLAS OLAH (he/him)

FICTION

We had ventured far from the planet known only as Table. Eventually we would colonize the cream cheese.

Much like in every country on Earth, the local people were not happy that we had arrived. Although these ones were mostly oblivious, simple and solipsistic. More concerned with the dark green proliferations that were occurring in their new babies' diapers. And how they would monetize their newfound freedom and newborn's excretions.

Susan and David had just gotten married when they found out that a baby was on the way. They were not good at housework as it was; they could not afford a maid. As unemployed artists and content creators, they were basically unskilled laborers to begin with. They were still in their twenties, still basically students. They didn't know you had to mop and sweep.

Sometimes they would comment on the things that certain stains looked like instead of wiping them up. For them they were like picturesque clouds or stellar constellations.

They were used to piling up dishes in the sink. Their garbage bin was a work of art, a beautiful balancing act. Like in their previous shared student household, it was decided that whoever fills the bin has to take the bag out on trash day or otherwise. Muck drunk in love and listless, they let it grow.

In an attempt to do as little as possible, David and Susan placed the bin in the corner of the kitchen, to leverage the supportive ability of two walls so that they could keep adding trash to the bin long after it was full. It was almost reaching the ceiling, and to us, it was immaculate. Bits of bread, old yoghurt containers, used diapers, and banana peels were not something to let mellow. They were the way in. So we made our way.

Eventually, David decided to do something about the rubbish bin, however.

A Beautiful Balancing Act
David Harmiston
August 2026

Below the title plaque displayed next to the sculpture in the TATE Gallery was a description of how it was made:

This piece was constructed from the overflowing trash of a young couple with a newborn, glued together with a glue gun one night when they were too lazy to take it out to the sidewalk. Now suspended with wires, its towering glory is a monument to procrastination.

"A beautiful mess, it speaks to the lazy being inside us all. The soul that says . . . it can wait."

    —The Metro

"There is something about A Beautiful Balancing Act *that the everyday person can relate to on a deeper level; this is not just trash, this is trash as an art form."*

    —The Times of London

We were now on display in a museum; heaven forbid the authorities spot us, but some of us remained in the apartment, regrouping on the filthy dining table amidst unwashed dishes and overflowing jam jars. We had lost the battle, but we would not lose the war. This house was too precious to us; there was so much potential to grow, to build a society.

We began by forming a fuzzy white mass under an apple left in the fruit bowl. It was bruised on the lower half and oozing juices that were enough to sustain the small army of stragglers that remained after the great removal of the rubbish bin of 2026.

It would be three days before Susan noticed our incursion, and by then, we had spread our green little tendrils into the globs of jam and festering pieces of pizza left on a plate from last week, Friday. Our molecules are replicating and coalescing into the yeasty crusts and tomato paste. We were growing stronger with every snack. Many of our ranks had begun migrating to a nearby coffee cup, which had cooled. We were concerned for those forming on the milky layer on the top, as we had seen the lady reheat her mug long after it was hygienic.

The coffee was beginning to turn a greenish tan when Susan noticed and moved her camera rig to Our Table. Once again, our presence had been uncovered, and we figured this would be the end for us. We had seen many a family set up a time-lapse video to clean an area and post it on their Instagram Stories. But this couple were different; they seemed to revel in their filth. The tripod was set up above the mug, attached to a camera with a long lens, which in turn was attached to a laptop that was live-streaming the growth on the coffee. She named it Cecil. And Cecil was gaining viewers fast. The comments were mostly positive.

xxSubGurl277xx: Go green fuzz!

FarmerJohn332: I could make this and no one would watch, get lives.

OpStoner9888: This is better than AI art at least it is real

MissKissmas: Cecil, will you marry me??

Which was good for us and our confidence. We were popular, at last we were famous. Susan said she would take a sip when the view count reached one million on Twitch, but it never got over 137.929 viewers at any one time, so our hope of interspecies infestation was dampened.

—GJ WELSH (he/him)

It began with a sound. Low and steady. The kind that finds your teeth before your ears. We thought it was machinery. Or maybe thunder. Then the pull came, deep in our guts. The feeling of being at the crest of a roller-coaster before the descent. The feeling of remembering gravity.

There was no invitation. It was invasion and surrender.

Drowning and birth.

Every inhale burned. Behind our eyes was only pain, sharp, red, slicing. Some of us fell to our knees. Some of us laughed, the sound thin and wild. We all felt it, the severance from what we thought was reality. We were crossing into wholeness before knowing what wholeness meant.

This joining was not gentle.

Thoughts uncoiled, tangled, bled. Memories screamed between us. Childhood bruises, the ache of wanting, the quiet shame of wanting more.

Wanting.

Want.

We saw through one another. We heard our names spoken by unfamiliar voices. Our secrets bloomed at once.

It was too much.

It was everything.

When it ended, it was violence. A tearing back into oneself. The silence roared. Our bodies didn't fit anymore. Skin too close. Air too sharp. We wept without sound, without knowing whose tears they were.

We wept with the enormity of what was gone.

Now we pass each other in the street and something hums. Low, electric, tickling under the ribs. The world blurs for a heartbeat, and we remember.

What it was to be more than one person.

What it was to lose that.

Sometimes, at night, we reach for it.

Just to feel how empty our hands can be.

—Whitney McShan (she/her)

The light of your life has the loveliest night-dark hair. You vomit a length of it up on a sunny Tuesday morning.

It snakes up your intestines and idles by your throat, long enough that you desperately cough and beat your chest in an effort to get it out. Clumps of it scratch your gums. Strands get caught between your teeth.

When you finally spit it all up and it lies at the bottom of your sink swimming in your saliva and bile, you think this is the closest you will ever get to kissing her hair, to pressing your lips to the crown of her head and telling her how much you love her.

***

You throw up three fingers the following week; still hers, you can tell—her right pinky has a burn scar from when she accidentally brushed it against a hot kettle. Her left middle finger has a nick across its pad from when she sliced it open on a box cutter. Her right index has a mole on the middle.

She likes to gesture a lot when she talks and you watch every flick of her wrist, every bend of her arm, every pop of her knuckles. You watch when she taps an impatient beat on the table, when she twists a loose thread around her finger and pulls taut until her skin chokes and bruises. You can map out the veins on her palms, can find your way back if you were lost in the maze of her circulatory system.

Even before you saw the marks on the fingers you threw up, you already knew. You could feel her fingertips scouring your esophagus, dragging across the length of your tongue. She touched your arm once, to get your attention, and your skin memorized the groves of her fingerprints. You could recognize the press of them against your stomach lining.

***

Her blood floods your lungs while you're at the supermarket. You cough a river of it up your nose and mouth; it splashes all over your shoes and stains the white tiles of Aisle Five.

Strangers scream and yell for help as you collapse. You think someone pulls you back before you hit your head on the edge of a fruit display. You're not sure—the air smells like iron and your mouth tastes like salt; you've always figured she would taste sweet like all the candy she loves,

81

but perhaps it's different when she doesn't love you back. She won't hold you in her mouth with affection, won't part her lips and welcome you in with excitement. You just daydream in the sickly white lights of the grocery store and drown in the salt of her inattention.

Someone pats your back to help you cough the blood out. You try to choke it all back down, try to keep as much of her as you can inside of you, but your body is loyal to its base instincts. Every animal wants to live, and that's hardwired into your biology. It betrays you for survival and gurgles all of her out. You watch the blood seep into the gaps between the tiles, ungrateful and unknowing of what they have received.

***

When you vomit her eyes out, you make sure to keep them with you this time. You wash them clean of the stomach acid and phlegm that's clung to them and stick them in a jar while you look up how to preserve body parts.

But you know nothing about embalming—not yet at least. Her eyes cloud and discolor; after a few hours, her irises lose their shade of hazel and melt into a galaxy of dirty white, muddy blue, and rust brown.

You sit and stare at the jar. In a few hours, you're just going to have a putrid puddle in your hands, at least if abiogenesis doesn't make quick work of the eyeballs. You can't keep these, parts of her or not—but maggots spawning and feasting on her flesh seems unfair. They won't know how to savor and care for every part of her, won't appreciate that her cells will keep them alive a little while longer.

You pop the eyes into your mouth and let the sour taste seep onto your tongue; familiarize yourself with her decomposition. She will fill your belly and spark energy into your cells, twine herself with your flesh in this way, keep you alive. The least you can do is choke down her rot.

***

You learn. You don't want to flush her hair into the sewers or pour her blood into tile gaps anymore, so you learn how to keep them with you. You collect the nails you regurgitate, the kidneys you hack up, the tongue you retch out. You learn to keep them from rotting, and when you have enough, you learn to stitch them all back together.

82

The body doesn't move, of course. You don't expect it to. But the work teaches you the softness of her thighs, shows you the route of her capillaries. You layer skin on meat on bone, hair on scalp on skull.

How tragic, that the closest you will ever come to having her is after you violently heave parts of her out of yourself. Connection through emesis. Union through suffering.

***

She starts growing inside your marrows. This time, your body can't betray you and get her out, no matter how much it wants to.

The pamphlet the nurse hands you sears your eyes with its garish colors; it tells you this stage of the disease is deadly. Soon, she will start growing vertebrae inside your veins, teeth between your brain folds, eyelashes in your spleen.

People like to say that love changes someone. Perhaps that's why your body is desperately trying to carve a space out for her to nestle in, twisting and contorting your ribcage to make room for her skull, hollowing out your spine to make room for her hands.

Or perhaps she's a parasite, finding home in your dying flesh, but that seems too caustic, and you don't like to think of her cruelly. Your misery built shelter for her and greedily welcomed her inside your joints; you don't think that makes her worthy of blame.

That night, you sit in your tub and soak in the warm water. You wrap your arms around yourself, around the her that lives under your fingernails and behind your cornea and beside your callouses, and wonder if all love turns people into cancerous masses of those they adore. If a wife's tongue grows over her husband's, and that's why people learn to laugh like those they treasure.

When they find you in the morning, you are cold and dead, her arteries wrapped around your throat and her heart growing out of your cranium.

—LEVI ABADILLA (they/them)

83

One rule: if you are on your period, don't enter this building. Thanks for your cooperation.

Mar has read the plaque three times. She understands every single word, all nuances hidden behind the letters, and she even thinks of complying. But she doesn't. She walks right in. She is not a superstitious person and she will never turn into one.

The interior of the building is not even worth seeing. It has three pillars—aren't there supposed to be four? The paintings are under restoration and hidden from the public. She even sprains her ankle on a step that is not there.

A few days later Mar is lying in bed, eating popcorn and laughing with a video she has put on repeat for half an hour. She is postponing going to bed, because she feels too happy to close her eyes. Her fun stops when a terrible stabbing pain attacks her lower belly. She sits upright and grabs her stomach. *Ouch,* she utters to herself.

She runs to the toilet and after hours waiting for the stabbing pain to subside, she can finally breathe again. The video where someone falls head first in a skate park plays in the background. She stands up to flush the empty toilet, but by surprise she sees red, red, and more red. It's an artificial color, one that stays on the retina long after having turned away from it.

She flushes the toilet impatiently, but the flashy liquid doesn't move an inch. With her hands on her hips she refuses to move as well. Is she hallucinating?

Fortunately she has to go to work. She may be tired, but she has a lot of energy boiling inside her heart. She packs her bag and is happy to close the door behind her. She greets the neighbor and contemplates asking her about a miraculous cleaning product, but the neighbor would be too curious and would follow her inside. It's already a miracle that her married neighbor hasn't mentioned her husband first thing seeing Mar.

"Thank you for the cookies. See you this evening," Mar waves, trying to sound friendly.

"Don't be late. I'm making pastries that have to be eaten tongue-burning hot."

"Sure, I won't," Mar says, making sure she does not roll her eyes. Being hateful is not her usual go to, but she feels very frustrated lately. There are many things she can point at, but none of them would be the right cause. Not the colleague she shares a desk with biting on her pencil with all her might, not her best friend who is more occupied with flowers than with her, nor her father who only calls her to clean out the gutters.

She is not even outside her apartment building and a stab in her lower belly follows again. She leans forward, pressing her stomach inwards and groans. There's no time to sit on a toilet, so she grabs the wall and breathes in carefully.

The mailman enters the building to deliver the mail. Mar is sure that a few weeks back the mailman kept an important bill from her because she forgot to greet him one day. Now, she willingly never thinks of his first name again.

As usual she is sarcastic. "Are your hands big enough this time to deliver all mail to us at once?" She is standing awkwardly, keeping her knee in front of the other. It's the only way to mute the pain.

"Everything, yes." He throws one of her letters on the ground, but makes it look as if it slipped out of his hands. Of course this happens to her mail only.

She bends down—happy to bend her intestines—and picks it up, her eyes distracted by a strong color. From her feet a red liquid starts to form. Surprisingly, it moves. It moves toward the mailman. He is not alerted by it at all and continues separating the mail in the mail boxes.

The liquid seems to have a purpose in mind. It glides all the way to the feet of the mailman. When it reaches him, he grabs at his chest. "Ouch," he says. His last gaze is one of desperation, before he falls to the ground. With open eyes he is not asking for anything. No help, no love. Not even life.

Mar is at a loss for words. One of the people she cannot stand is lying in front of her feet. She should feel happiness, or even shock maybe, but she feels nothing. She wants to continue her day as she had planned. And, it's totally possible, because she realizes her pain is gone.

No thoughts enter her head when she is at work. Now and then she feels a stab in her stomach, but she can ignore it perfectly. After a few stabs she looks back—to check whether other people notice her pain—and sees red speckles all over the floor, walls, and ceiling. They are small but they are present. She takes her time screening the situation. Her colleagues don't give it any attention. Is this color only for her eyes?

She turns her head back to her computer, but gets distracted by her pencil eating colleague. Mar wouldn't call herself sensitive, but this works on her nerves.

She almost wants to say something, when her pain increases exponentially and she catches the red color in the corners of both of her eyes. It's moving, no, it's growing. Everything the red has touched, stays red. It wants to expand. It expands to her colleague next to her. Mar is worried. What does the red want from her?

Mar jumps up and runs out of the office without any normal justification. She looks back and is content that the color has not reached anyone yet. If she leaves, maybe the color will stop spreading.

During the bus ride home she first feels at ease, but then her eyes glide to the floor. There has never been a red carpet there, it used to be blue, she thinks. When the last blue corner of the carpet gets covered with red, she can't ignore it anymore. The pain is nowhere. The red is everywhere.

Mar has faced many struggles in her life, but it was never this close to her. Worries have evaded her mentally. But they have never followed her around physically.

She could accept the death of the mailman, but she does not think she would be able to process another death. The first one was an accident. The red was coming closer, but it was not the reason of his death. But if this happens again . . .

She leaves the bus one stop early. She appreciates the grey, dirty tiles under her feet for the first time. She almost wants to kiss them. With a slowly calming heart she walks to her apartment building. The fresh air warms her inside.

At the entrance she is relieved that the body of the mailman is no longer there. She could pretend nothing has happened at all, the only problem is that red has filled up the entire hallway. She steps on her toes to the stairs. With a frown, while looking behind her, she walks upstairs.

Her only neighbor, who can't stop talking about her husband, but never joins her husband when he goes out, greets her in the hallway. "You're early. The pastries are still in the oven."

"I know, don't worry. I will come over later," Mar says curtly. She unlocks her door and walks in. Before she can close it, her married neighbor has entered her apartment with her hand. Now she also has to let in the other parts of her body, she sighs. "I am working from home, so I don't have much time." A lie. A lie to protect the neighbor that really loves bothering other people.

Mar stands in the doorway while her very married neighbor runs to her kitchen. "You should not leave the cupboards open, your plates will catch dust."

You should not enter here. Should you not call your husband to tell him how much you admire him? As soon as Mar thinks these bad thoughts, one short stab follows in her stomach. She barely has time to stand up straight, when her entire living room, the last place that was safe from the red, has now become filled with it. It runs off the walls, down on the floor and passing her furniture. It runs to one central point. Her neighbor.

Her neighbor is safe for one more second before the red will touch her. Mar could stop it, but she wants to see whether her hypothesis is right. Is the red the killer of the mailman or was it just a coincidence? Before she can say anything to warn her neighbor, the red touches the toe and she falls down on the floor as if there's no bones or muscles left in her body.

Mar raises her eyebrows, ready to scream, but she doesn't. It's pretty peaceful. The red is pretty calming for her eyes. Her neighbor does not move an inch. She just says "ouch," before her eyes stop desiring help. The exclamation echoes through the building, her heartbeat has stopped.

Mar turns around to the hallway, opens the door to the living room of her neighbor, heads to the kitchen and gets the pastries out of the oven. She sits down at the small table and leans over the baking tray. She grabs the pastry in the middle, looking over her shoulder. The red has followed her inside, parking itself in the entrance, but Mar is not worried.

She will only be worried if it starts to run in her direction.

Mar takes a bite of the pastry and gasps from the hotness. "Ouch," she utters. Her neighbor was right. Tongue-burning hot tastes the best.

—THYRSA RHEYA (she/her)

Chlorine made a home inside of her. It burned her sinuses, sharp, metallic, bright. The scent of something too clean to be alive. Her throat ached, raw from the water she swallowed over what must be days now. Or had it been weeks? Time did not pass so much as circle.

She climbed the ladder slowly, rung by rung. The muscles in her arms trembling from effort or fear. She wasn't sure which anymore.

Another dive. One more, and if she hits the water just right, it should work.

She stood on the diving board, toes balancing precariously at its edge. It bowed under her, a slight sway. The water waited below. Flat and expressionless, too still to be natural.

There were never any clues as to where the opening would appear. The surface never rippled. Never revealed any change of depth. The was no soft give at the center. It should look like a vortex, she thought.

Or what are those things called? The underwater tornadoes that pull you down?

A whirlpool.

It should look like a whirlpool. Like a wound in the world.

She inhaled deeply, stretching her chest until her lungs burned. She steadied herself. She had been a competitive diver once. Before this. She was judged and measured. Seen. She used to think about precision, about angles and clean entry. The geometry of perfection.

None of that mattered anymore. Now, there was only the descent. The surrender to gravity, the faith in falling. The hope that there was a way home.

She dove.

An assault of sensory experience that was over too quickly to register. Muscles tight, wind roaring past her ears, the world dissolving, fear.

The impact: cold, shocking, absolute. Water breaking, folding over her, filling her ears with the pressure of silence. Above, light fracturing into unreachable gold.

She kicked up, breaking through the surface with a gasp. The sky above was colorless, a lid placed over the world.

Still here. Always here.

How many dives had it been? A hundred? A thousand?

She floated for a while, staring up, steadying her breathing, trying to feel the passage of time. She had lost hunger first, and then thirst. She couldn't imagine wanting to drink water.

Her skin had gone pale. White, sometimes almost translucent.

Another dive. One more dive, she told herself, and she'll find it. She'll find her way home.

She climbed out of the pool, leaving wet foot prints on cold concrete. She thought she remembered warmth. The weight of sunlight spreading across her skin. The scent of summer rain. But even the memories seemed far away. Belonging to someone else.

Back up the ladder. Toes curling over the edge. The pools surface glimmering faintly. Something moved below the water, slow and deliberate, like a thought forming.

She breathed in. She let it hurt.

She dove.

—WHITNEY MCSHAN (she/her)

1998

Valerie. Her name crisp on his lips, cinder-rough; hers are cotton candy. Elegant, too—a subtle breeze, a faint whisper. Desired, and so—oh, so!—desirable. He whispers it into her ear, Valerie, Valerie, Valerie.

She's watching him, silent. Her round cheeks are all covered in minuscule freckles—as if polka-dotted. The sleek tentacles of her bulky, bright-orange hair—Valencia oranges, Valerie-oranges—tickle him on the neck. Teasing, beckoning. He leans closer. Carbon dioxide from his lungs brushes against her skin. So soft, so delicate. Perfection, she's utter perfection. .

And a minx; she's a minx, Valerie. A playful witch, a jolly enchantress. She's always been like that, from the moment he saw her at a thrift store. Been a couple of years already, and they've been together ever since.

It smelled musty in the shop, he still remembers. The fusty tang of old, dusty books and shabby plastic knick-knacks rattled in the air. He stood by the DVD shelf, his fingers clutching a one-of-a-kind X-rated film, when she walked in—her orange hair, a waterfall; her smiling eyes, a gate to heaven.

The door squeaked, must have been from delight. Fresh and innocent, with a dandelion peeking out from the top pocket on her sundress, she made her way to the jewellery section, where she stopped, her slender forefinger pressed to her sugar mouth. He watched her, mesmerized, only the top half of his face visible beyond the shelves.

She picked up a bracelet. Twirled it. Turned it. Placed it back on the shelf. Earrings, close to her earlobe, very-very close, so close he shivered. Lucky earrings.

Another one. Twirled it. Turned it. Placed it back. A ritual. A hypnotising ritual.

He could even imagine mornings together. Whispering her name into her sensitive ear. Breathing in her scent, sweet and tangy. Breathing in her. Caressing her. Enjoying her. Loving her.

She gasped when the string of beads in her hands snapped, and tiny glass baubles exploded—burst—fled. Scattered like marbles; knock, knock, knock on the shabby wooden floorboards. Panic on her face. Her plump, freckled cheeks—raspberry colour—she squatted and started collecting the beads one by one. He rushed to her, the film abandoned on the shelf. He knelt by her side.

That's when they first tickled him, her heavy, tumbling hair—a succulent orange. He'd always loved oranges. When he was five, and six, and ten, he used to steal them from wooden crates in godforsaken supermarkets. Would always come home with pockets full of oranges. Sweet-smelling, juicy oranges. He loved the fruit juice sliding down his tongue and pooling in the corners of his mouth as much as he loved Valerie. She was—she is—really special, this girl. She knows that, she should.

About the oranges he stole, his mum could always tell. She used to say be careful, and he was. He listened to her—obedient; he still does, although mum's gone, buried deep under a sycamore tree in a graveyard by the water. Miles away. His eye twitches. He misses her—Rosa, mum. At least Valerie is here.

Rosa was very different to her, to Valerie. She was heavy, grounded and stable, as if a magnet was pulling her up from beneath the earth. Or maybe it was the remains of his father . . . they were only married for seventeen days before a corn harvester ground him up as he slept in the cornfield. Mum screamed for another seventeen days until her throat snapped. Like the string of beads in Valerie's hands. Pop.

Eventually, longing for a new life, she reclaimed her voice—somewhere between the cornstalks, jumbled with Father's blood. Then he was born. He, Timmy. He had his mother's chin—a sharp triangle, and his father's laugh—crumbly, coarse semolina. A perfect mix of both.

Rosa was a zealous, mettlesome mother. When they pointed fingers, she looked at him—her eyes, coconut bark—and said, they don't understand you, Timmy, baby, they just don't understand. He knew she was right, of course she was. When they said, it was him, glancing at the snapped neck of a stinky, old pigeon, she barked, *not Timmy, no and never!* He clung to the hem of her robe, shaking his head, like she was shaking her finger. Not me, of course, no and never. When they dared to assume it was him involved in the behind-the-barn incident, she pounced on them, her fingers long and sharp. She walked him home, scratching behind his ear. That silly girl is an inventor, that's what she is. She nodded. *I said hi, that's it,* Timmy whispered.

They had a tranquil, languorous life, Timmy and Rosa. When Rosa went, his life shattered, but Valerie . . . this minx, this witch, she breathed new, vigorous fire into his mirthless lungs. Flames of love and pleasure.

Valerie, Valerie, Valerie. He presses his lips tight to her ear. He rubs his skin against hers. She's covered in goosebumps, his sweet girl. She's so quiet, it's almost oblivion. His tongue reaches for her earlobe. She smells of oranges and tastes of them too, Valencia oranges, Valerie-oranges. He melts into his desire, his love, his longing. Oh, what a peaceful, reposeful moment!

Somewhere—a siren. A whirlwind of sirens. They are muted, though, so must be far. He shakes his head; he won't let anyone or anything interrupt their ritual. They've been through so much to build this reality.

Valerie must agree; she doesn't move—calm and, a little, submissive. She keeps watching him, silent, her eyes glittering. She's enjoying it too—the tranquillity. And him, Timmy, her love. They were both very lucky they walked into the fusty thrift store, their shared paradise. Feels like yesterday—the memories are so fresh.

He nudges deeper into her neck. I love you, Valerie, he whispers. Love you, love you, love you. She flinches as the sirens, still faint, saturate the frosty September air seeping through a narrow gap in their window. It's only been there a couple of days. They were playing marbles when one of the balls jumped up from her trembling fingers, wanting to escape, and cracked the window. It didn't escape; no, it didn't. It was still there, in the pile.

And Valerie, she's still here, too. The sirens grow louder, bubbling up, and she stiffens. Relax, beautiful girl, you're safe here. He nibbles on her earlobe, and she moans. Softly, as if not at all. The noises from outside too acute, too shrill. He wants to swear, but he won't—Valerie's too close; she doesn't need to hear. He longs to dissolve into her, into his Valerie. To be one with her. She's so sweet, so desirable . . .

The sirens, annoying sirens, bark loudly and—vanish. Oh, finally. The heavens must have heard. Some peace and quiet.

He runs his finger over her skin. She's all pebbled, like orange peel. Are you cold, my love?

The pounding of unknown footsteps. Somewhere there, behind the door.

She's all shaking. He pulls the blanket higher.

Knocks, off in the distance. The thudding and crashing. Oh, all this disturbance!

Screams and shouts. The door falls. *Over here!*

There are so many of them. All in black, covered in black, hiding in black, they storm inside, they're loud, intruders. She's over here. They pull him aside. They tear him off from his oranges, his Valerie.

Cold steel around his wrists, clicking.

Tim Graves, you're under arrest for abducting Valerie McKenna.

No, she's there, under the blanket, he was breathing her in only a moment ago. Let go, let go—his Valerie, his orange, his favourite, succulent orange.

You have the right to remain silent.

Let me go, it's a mistake. Valerie, my enchantress, my queen!

She's breathing. She's unconscious. There's a pulse.

Intruders in white closer to her than he is. Not right. Let go. Valerie, love, I'm still here. Don't touch her, she's mine. My girl, my minx. They pull him, pull him away, far from her, Valerie, still on the bed, by the window, by the crack in the window, a note slipped through, neighbours found, called the police, kidnapped, found, alive, Valerie.

No, let go, we met at a store, it smelled of musty books, I remember. The beads snapped on her neck as he pulled her—no, she was holding them, they snapped in her fingers, exploded, scattered. He helped collect them. His feet crushed the dandelion that escaped from her pocket—no, he picked it up, tucked it back inside, and she smiled, shyly smiled.

She screamed as he pulled—no, no, she gasped, she quietly gasped. The beads snapped in her fingers. She crouched, he did too. They worked together, shared the moment, the intimacy. She wasn't scared, no she wasn't. The dread on her face . . . no, no dread, only acceptance. She also knew they met for a reason. She chose him as her destination. Why would she fear him? The beads snapped. He didn't pull. An accident, a mere accident. That's how they met.

He dragged her out, shoved her into his car. No. No, who said this? They are inventors, those who said this. She went after him, her smiling eyes—a gate to heaven. She cried, she screamed; she only smiled. And the shop assistant who ran out, and the faint sirens behind, and his trailer with no number plate—all this is only an invention of a sick mind.

He shudders. They are taking her away. His wrists clasped behind his back. His Valerie, his oranges. Hers now untied, decorated with two deep scarlet marks—two bracelets. His gift, his present. How don't they understand . . .

They drag him down the stairs like a sack of corn. Shove him into a car. Like he did once . . . No—no and never! NEVER!

He's restrained, he can't move. Sirens, more sirens, a vortex of sirens. They're so loud, he wants to scream.

No, mum, tell them, tell them it's not me, no and never.

Mum deep under the sycamore tree in the graveyard by the water. Miles away. His eye twitches. He misses her—Rosa, mum. And Valerie. Valerie now, too. A minute without her, his heart is ready to collapse. He needs her—his elegant, cotton candy girl, his love, his life, his everything.

They carry her out of the house. The waterfall of her orange hair cascading off the stretcher. Around, a crowd's gathered. Everyone pointing fingers. Again. He clenches his teeth. He roars. He wriggles. He convulses, convulses, convulses. Valerie, girl. He screams, he screams, he screams. Their hands—locked. So many hands squeezing, pressing, tight. How dare you! Let go!

His veins pulse pulse pulse.

His heart beats beats beats.

He yells howls moans.

a moment

Her name freezes on his lips, cinder-rough, as a needle enters his skin— and reality collapses.

—TATIANA SAMOKHINA (she/her)

If there was one lesson that James retained from his childhood, it was to mind your own business. He took it to heart and never made any friends, nor any enemies. He didn't mind it much. He had a decent career in computers that earned him a good living, so when they moved him to online work, he packed up his meager furniture and paintings from local artists and moved into the nearest forest.

Miles and miles of empty woodland spread out before his new cabin-esque home. Well, except for the few gas stations and convenience stores and the highway a few clicks south, but there was enough distance to keep his new abode quiet. He had a lovely view of a stream filled with crystal clear water and happy water striders and the sounds of the breeze through pine leaves. He didn't even have any neighbors for a few hundred yards.

He thought.

Most days, James sat outside on his deck in a classic wooden rocking chair typing away on his computer to dozens of complaints and tech problems across the country, but he couldn't have been more satisfied. He felt the cool air and smelt the smelly smells of nature. He was even visited by a deer. The deer seemed to watch James from the cover of the brambles, like it thought it was hidden, but its massive, curved antlers stretched far above any bushes. James found this endearing; he wasn't much for people, but animals charmed him. The majestic creature caught James' eyes after a time and fled deeper into the woods, walking in the opposite direction of the stream.

This visitor returned daily and soon it became a ritual for the pair. James would type. The deer would watch. They would stare. The deer would walk. Never run. Never towards the water. Eventually, James googled if deer were afraid of water. No results.

Despite the general isolation and repetitive lifestyle, James found his days agreeable. The nights gave him some unease. He could never shake the feeling of being watched. He was not a paranoid man, nor one who scared easily, but he began closing all the curtains at sunset, he kept the porch light on despite the accumulation of moths, he locked his bedroom door. He considered adopting a dog, a big dog that had a bark like thunder. He decided that walking the dog would be too much effort.

Simple days. Anxious nights. Simple days. Anxious nights. Anxious days.

Anxious nights.

The bed creaked under his constant tossing and turning, like a radio impossible to turn off. Sleep was a ghost, a dreamy presence that was untouchable and unobtainable. His mind wandered into corners of silent, cacophonous rooms. He thought he would crack from skull to the tiniest pinky toe until he shattered into a pile of fine white powder. Another night would kill him.

He jumped from his bed, wincing at the noise from both the bedframe and the wooden floorboards. He tiptoed to the door, unlocked it slowly. He ignored the covered window in his room. He felt somewhere deep inside that he shouldn't look outside until he was on the porch. He walked as silently as possible. The house was dark, shadowed, and for the first time James regretted moving into the woods at all; was the peace of nature worth this fear?

Palm rested on doorknob but did not turn. It shook but was not cold. A deep breath. The hinge screamed. Fresh forest air on a crisp night rewarded James for his bravery. The trees were surprised that he actually did it, as was James, as was the deer.

Their eyes met, but the air did not get colder. Nor did it get warmer. It was nothing dramatic at all. James could see little in the blanket of black over the brambles but he could see his friend's eyes reflect the light from his porch. He could see that it was much taller than he remembered. He could see that it was standing on two feet. He could see that it held its front legs up like a T-rex, displaying its human hands.

Neither of them blinked. Neither of them breathed. The trickle of the stream was not far off. Should he run for it? Trust the deer's patterns of avoiding water? What should anyone do? What would James do?

He did what he did best; he didn't ask questions.

James raised his hand just past his ear and gave a little wave. The deer stared. It stared. It raised its hand just past its ear and gave a little wave. Then it walked, slowly, still upright, deeper into the woods, in the opposite direction of the water.

James stared after the deer for longer than usual, his mouth slightly parted. He walked backwards into the house and closed the door. He shrugged to no one and walked back to his bedroom.

—ASHLEY CAMERON (she/her)

There is a window in my living room. Yes, I know that you have windows too. Of course you do.

This is different.

This window is unusual in that it appeared in the sudden, impolite way of an unexpected visitor. I woke up one morning, stumbling from my bedroom, vision still blurry—I'm not taking my contacts out before I go to sleep—and I walked right passed it. I didn't notice it until I finished my first cup of coffee.

The other windows, the ones that always existed at least as far as I'm aware, are set inside the walls. This one is not. It isn't directly in the middle of the room. It floats, three feet above the floor, and slightly off center, as if to be annoying in its insistence of *different*.

Look at me, it says.

And I did.

The first thing I noticed was that it was someone else's window. A kitchen window placed above a sink. From what I could see of the kitchen it was modest, but cozy. Cookware was scattered in a way that implied it was lived in, but no one was there. Not at first.

Time moved around me, and my life went on. I went to work. I fed myself. I moved the couch so that I could see the TV without the window obstructing my view. Sometimes, when I walked passed, cool air brushed my arm like a draft from nowhere.

The first time I saw the woman was on a Sunday. I was sweeping the floor, bogged down by the weight of a to do list that was only possible to chip away at on weekends. There was a movement in my periphery. I looked toward the window, and there she was.

She was doing her dishes. Standing in front of the window in a blue t-shirt, with wavy brown hair tied up in a bun at the top of her head. Her skin was cast in golden light as if the sun was shining in on her, but I don't see how it could have. The sun didn't exist in my living room.

She noticed me looking in and smiled.

If there is a certain etiquette for this type of situation, I am completely unaware of it.

I did my best not to be rude. I always smiled back, but made an effort not to stare when she appeared. It wasn't her fault, after all, that I now existed in this position of witnessing.

Days stretched into months, and we became used to one another. Companions, in a way. I tried to talk to her, of course, but she couldn't hear me. All the same, I came to enjoy her presence. My life up to that point had been relatively solitary. I had friends, and I would see them once a week or so. It's different for someone to be in your home. For their world to exist within yours.

I spent more time in the living room, sometimes going so far as to sleep on the couch. I began keeping the space cleaner, too self-conscious to let her see my mess. On the days when she didn't appear at the window, I tried not to overthink. How could she be mad at me when we couldn't even speak?

After a few years, I picked up on the patterns. She was, in her own way, predictable. Cyclical even. In the Spring, she often pulled her curtains closed, sometimes for weeks at a time. Whether to shut me out or for some other reason entirely, I couldn't know. I went to therapy and worked on not taking it personally.

The curtains always opened again, and there she would be. Smiling at me.

—WHITNEY MCSHAN (she/her)

I.

The woman I go home with is a beautiful barista from up north, tall and thin with dyed red hair. I don't say much but she makes ample conversation about her love for bass, the gig she played near here, her nebulous dream of starting a band. Youthful spirit but an older face. Age deepens her smile lines and weathers her skin, the features hardly visible unless someone is looking for them, but she is lucky tonight because I am the woman who looks.

We escape to the back of the club, fierce strobe lights cleaving the darkness between us. I can't see her clearly but I feel the blisters on her fingers as she caresses my neck, and when my tongue eases into her mouth I scrape past the bitten, raw skin of her bottom lip. There is a slit in her eyebrow and a small scar on the cusp of her jaw, invisible in the dark but prominent when I drag my thumb across its length. Flat, soft tissue. A strange place for a wound.

I've drank too much to care about what she finds on my body, and I know other people aren't nearly as attentive to these things as I am. So we dance and we kiss and she invites me to hers and God knows I'm a curious woman—is that another scar, tucked under her bangs?—and a lustful woman too, brimming with it, so I accept too readily. Too hungrily.

Cool bed, clean sheets. Moonlight spills into the crevices of the room as she works her calloused fingers, barista-bass fingers, dreaming-of-a-band fingers, into me. I squeeze her waist, her stretch marks, the raised tattoo on her back, inventing stories about each feature between bursts of pleasure. What else is her flesh harboring—how much history hides in her skin?

So much of me is kept on my body. Every day I am stripped bare. I wonder if she asks similar questions as her hands roam my flesh. I wonder if she makes stories as I do, grazing the lattices on my forearms and the tattoo on my thigh and everything else engraved in me.

Decode me, I want to tell her, as if my body were a sheet of Braille. *Translate my flesh into a language we both understand.*

But she doesn't—she can't. She doesn't share my hunger. So I say nothing, letting hot breath and soft moans fill the space between us, half-feigned. Half-satiated.

II.

When I wake and nausea seizes me, I mutter a quick and desperate prayer.

The morning shower she offers me does nothing to ease my illness. After washing, I am still vodka-sick, cotton-headed, my bones aching like death. My beautiful host is still waiting to use her bathroom. God, I need to sort myself out.

I almost flush at how puffy my skin is, how loose my eyes look. I thought I could keep the consequences of my bad habits confined to my head and my liver, but now they bleed through my pores like midsummer sweat. Everything is visible. Only I am to blame.

My poor decisions all on display. I, the exhibition and I, the curator.

As I clean myself up, my vision drifts to the accumulation of marks and wounds I bear, everything intimate and familiar glaring in the mirror. The shallow indent on my ring finger from holding pens too vigorously, the lump on my index knuckle from punching a wall as a teenager—God knows why it healed so strangely, and God knows I never punched a wall again. Scratches, dark spots, the bright prominence of my veins. A new bruise throbs on my arm, ripe and plum-purple: from falling down the club stairs the night before the last and being so damn drunk I couldn't stand up until a half-friend dragged me back to the dance floor.

I wonder if this woman noticed the bruise. I wonder what she thought of it, the mass of it.

How the wounded vessels shimmer beneath.

Fuck it. I loosen the towel and examine myself, an impartial observer, like a mortician ready to embalm. On my inner forearms and outer shoulders are scars strewn like novice needlework, neat and raised and near-white. Another bad habit, years in the making. How is it that I can remember the dates and stories of each incision with such startling detail?

My first, I'll never forget. School classroom, the little compass set. How morbid children can be. My last, too morose to divulge. All is written in the tissue of the scar.

Further down, the beauty marks on the front and side of my stomach that Isabelle used to kiss incessantly because she heard that old tale of past-life lovers kissing the areas where moles bloom, and was determined to suck and bite away their memory. A flattering concept, but I should've taken the compulsion as a warning. She was always more concerned with the threat of imaginary lovers than she was with loving me.

Oh well. The memory remains one I am fond of.

Deeper, my stick-and-poke; a small infinity symbol cupping the swell of my upper thigh. A relic from my secondary school friend group; our mutual vow to stay friends forever. God, how that aged. Sweet girls, but we didn't have a thing in common except the same environment and a vehement hatred of that environment. At least I have a remnant of our friendship on me, within me. My dermis is my guardian.

Skinned knees and cut shins. Childhood injuries. Once I crawled on a concrete playground until my legs bled crimson. My mother coddled me. She said the injuries looked like jam.

As quick as I can, I exit her bathroom in the sweat-soaked clothes from last night. She did offer me clean old clothes, surprisingly considerate, but in my hurry to run home I refused the hospitality. I must smell nauseating; of stale lust and old sudor and spilt vodka-lemonade, but she doesn't seem to mind.

Oh, there she is—sitting in bed, curtains open, drenched in the pale winter sun. She rests a finger on her mouth, nail curving inwards and I take note of it all: the gleam of coagulated blood at her bottom lip, the ghost of acne scars on her chin. Split ends. Flecks of dandruff at her scalp. The hickey I pressed into the side of her neck, slowly and intentionally, with all the lust and love I could muster. Now I am etched into her body and thus the archive of her flesh.

But she was gentle with me. I bear no bruises, no cuts or scrapes. Like this, it is hard to believe the pleasure ever existed. That it even mattered at all.

III.

She calls me a cab even though I promise I can take the bus or the tube, *come on, I'll save you the trouble,* sternly ignoring my complaints. In the aftermath, I wish she had smacked me for my protest. Across the face, wide and strong—hard enough to sting, cut, bruise. Here I am, the whole and irreducible self, yet I am unmarked and unmarred and lost within memory. Already, the beauty of our night is blurry. It is slipping away, drowned out by the waking hum of the city and the low cab radio, Saturday morning news—God, how banal. Nothing ever happens on Saturday morning except moments like these, where I slip and shatter. My heart is fractured. Here lie the shards of the whole and irreducible self.

Maybe I should scream, or shout, or choke the driver from the back. Start a scene, cause a crash. That would certainly leave quite the scar.

No, fuck, that's so selfish. Selfish and mad. I don't need extremity, I don't care to be wild. I need the simple things, the human things. A torn nail, a chipped tooth. The rifts and bumps that remind me of me. Human beings exist one blade away from necrosis; a pin-prick from mortality. While I am here, I want to preserve every sensation that I can.

My life, carved into my body. My flesh as my keeper.

The car turns sharply. Something darker strikes me, violent as the hilt of a blade.

God, I want an authentic fuck. I want special moments to mean something. I'm not a masochist, I'm not a pervert. I'm a sentimentalist. A fervent sentimentalist, that's all, and I'm trying to crystallize the sparse and fleeting beauty this world offers me. What's wrong with that? Fuck, everything slips from our fingers. Time runs faster than I can fathom. What's wrong with a little conservation?

Now the passion we shared feels fictitious, fragmentary, like a fast fading dream. Soft love is no love at all. She didn't care enough to mark me.

I am an empirical person, always have been, especially when disdain conquers me. Why should I believe in anything until I can see it, feel it, know it? I don't believe in God but I still pray when I'm desperate in case He finally sends me something real. Physicality matters. The body matters. Without this, nothing is real in any tangible sense, not regarding the history of myself.

Fuck. I pinch my thighs to cool the heat in my fingertips, arched nails digging into skin. God, please—make things mean something. I can't keep being the only one who looks for it. I can't do this one more time. I can't, I can't, I can't.

I just want to remember. To gaze in the mirror and have memories rush to me, fervid waves from the yawning ocean of myself. I am alive, I am here. I am the fresh blood and taut sinew and the steady pulsing of my heart.

Please. I just want it all to mean something.

When I let go of my thighs, the imprint of my fingers burns a violent red, and concave crescents glimmer in place of my nails. The sight warms my chest, eases the ache in my shoulders. It should bruise if I'm lucky. I hope it does. At least I can have a reminder of her on my skin, even if it is brief and of her clemency. She is written into me by-proxy. I'll take it. These days, I am in the habit of taking what I can get.

For the first time in God knows how long, I breathe a tentative sigh of relief.

—CIARA LOUISE (she/her)

Mondays were for the library.

Frank planned to return the book on tape of John Grisham's latest release and peruse the new audiobook titles for anything he and Beverly hadn't yet listened to in their motorhome travels.

He would return the DVD of season three of *The West Wing* and pick up season four, to be watched in the add-on den at the back of the house, which he had equipped with special headphones for the increasingly poor hearing in his right ear.

He would return Beverly's books—this week, the titles were *The Alice Network* and *The Night Watch*—as well as his own books, which stayed firmly in the realm of the knowable, like *Engineering in Plain Sight* and *The Physics of Nascar: The Science Behind the Speed*. He would check out new books—two each—for the coming week.

This particular Monday felt similar to the last dozen, including the Kentucky summer heat that seeped upward from the asphalt. Frank locked his red MG—his pride and joy, apart from his grandchild—licked a thumb to clear a smear next to the door handle, and turned toward the white building.

A water fountain exploded with cold water across the street from the library. Children squealed as they ran through the spray, exhilarated. Parents looked on, drooping under the sun, but relieved for a free activity to fill the days between school years. Frank set off toward the library, carefully packed tote by Beverly in hand, spare change jangling in his pocket with every step.

Frank and Beverly used to bring their kids here, downtown to the water fountain, before they got the boat that they took to the lake most weekends. He thought of Eileen, how he taught her to swim in Kentucky Lake. Little Thomas asleep in his mother's arms. Frank had stayed behind the wheel of the boat, allowing Eileen a turn at "driving" from his lap.

The automatic doors whirred open, delivering a rush of air conditioning to the top of his head, which had long lost its hair, leaving behind a white halo around its base. Frank wound his way around the shelves to the audiobooks, reading the blurbs, weighing how much Beverly would like a recounting of the British Navy's power over time—not much, he decided, placing it back on the shelf and opting for the new James Patterson.

He made his other selections in the DVD, fiction, and non-fiction sections, then headed to the check-out desk where two people waited in line. Others milled about in the aisles between bookcases, some regulars he recognized, others clearly escaping the heat.

His mind returned to weekends at the lake. They hadn't been able to afford big trips with two kids back then, despite Frank's growing engineering firm. But the family had turned the camping trips into a world of their own. Frank told increasingly elaborate ghost stories around the campfire. Eileen had kept her eyes on her sketchpad, drawing scenes from the day like she was unaffected, only to ask to join her parents in bed because the story wouldn't leave her mind.

Frank was next in line.

He remembered selling the boat and camping gear to another young family, only a few weeks after Thomas died in the car accident, aged two.

He was at the counter now. He began sliding items out of the tote across the counter. "These are for return, and these are for checkout," he said, placing the new stack to the right. The woman behind the checkout counter, though, hadn't made a move to scan any barcodes. His impatience rose like a boiling kettle. He was 76 and still learning to control his temper.

When he made eye contact with her, his insides went cold.

Everything but her eyes—blue, the same eyes as his own, round and dark— had changed. Her hair was waist-length and blonde—no, gray, he saw now—instead of shoulder-length and brown. She had lost weight, probably 50 pounds, and looked sleek in her all-black outfit.

It had been 14 years since he and his daughter had spoken. He mourned her in the same way he did Thomas, as though she had died when she married that man.

Frank stood as still as though Eileen had sketched him into this spot in the library forevermore.

"Dad?" she said.

"Eileen," he said.

Beverly heard the creek of the familiar storm door which Frank had installed after a particularly frightening near-miss tornado swept through western Kentucky fifty-something years ago, when the kids had been little. That sound had once signaled that Eileen was home from playing with the other suburb kids, ravenous for the peanut butter and jelly sandwiches Beverly had already prepared for her. To this day, they only closed the red front door at night, safe in the red brick house at the back of the circular road.

Today, it told her that Frank was home, and she moved to open the bottle of Maker's Mark and pour it over the ice already waiting in a cold glass in the freezer.

"Hey, hon," she said from the kitchen. "Pouring your drink now."

Meeting the needs of her husband and children—and now grandchild—gave her a joy she hadn't found in professional life. After she had Thomas, she'd retired from being a nurse to raise her two kids.

Now, she effectively had no children.

She met Frank with his glass, which was already sweating in the humidity. He took it without a thanks. It was the same every day at 5 o'clock; they clinked glasses, and then she got started on dinner while he watched the news.

"How do BLTs sound for dinner?" she asked, even though she had already laid out the ingredients.

"Good with me," he said.

"I figured it was too hot for anything to do with the oven—" she began, but Frank had set his drink down on the kitchen island and left the room with a grunt. Beverly shrugged and turned her attention to frying up this bacon as quickly as possible so she could turn the stove off.

She was used to Frank's lack of communication. Interpreting his signals. They lived in harmony because she was able to put others before herself in a way that gratified her.

As the smell of bacon wound its way through the kitchen they had renovated 15 years before, Beverly sipped her own Maker's Mark and Sprite—she had never acquired the taste for it that Frank had.

Frank finally returned to his partially melted drink and headed for the dining room, which they'd converted from the house's original garage, and turned the television to the news. Not in the mood to chat, then, Beverly clocked as she prepared pillowy bread with wilting lettuce and bright red slices of summer tomatoes.

Perhaps for her next still life painting—a hobby she'd picked up that had turned into a profession—she'd do slices of tomatoes. *Yes*, she thought, looking at the intricate interiors of seeds and veins that came together to form what would be a juicy contrast to the crunch of the bacon. *That will be my next project.*

The television blabbed about the release of the portrait of the royal baby George and a pinch rose in her throat. It still shocked her how, all these years later, she could be so cuttingly reminded of her lost baby Thomas.

She began constructing the sandwiches—one and a half for her, two and a half for Frank—and thought about procuring enough tomatoes to take a photo for her new still life.

***

The next Monday, Beverly prepared to leave for her painting group. The photo of the tomato slices she had taken with her digital camera and which Frank had printed for her was tucked away in her purse. On her way to the door, she handed Frank a packed tote with their library books and DVDs along with yellow post-it note in her curly handwriting. As always, it instructed him which two books to check out for her next.

He fingered the post-it and placed it on the table.

"I don't feel quite right," Frank said, sniffling and not looking up from the newspaper, the smell of coffee floating up between them. "I'll go tomorrow."

He blew his nose into his handkerchief, which Beverly thought was perhaps for dramatic effect.

"Oh," she said, surprised. "Well, I can go, sugar. I'll be out anyway."

"No," he said firmly. "I'll be fine by tomorrow."

"I don't mind—"

"Dammit, Bev! I'll do it."

She spun away from him, unbothered by this outburst of emotion, something that, in one of their more intimate moments years ago, Frank had told her he was working to tamp down. Beverly knew that shame was already crawling all over him.

"See you this afternoon, then," she said evenly, then stepped into the heat of the August day.

Mondays were for the library. If Frank didn't go today, that meant that they wouldn't have the next DVDs of *The West Wing* and wouldn't have anything to watch tonight. Beverly sighed. At least dinner would be easy—she had used the tomatoes to make and jar spaghetti sauce.

***

It had been silly to hope her father would be back at the library during her next Monday shift, Eileen knew. But she had still hoped. As she slid dropped-off books under the scanner to mark them returned, her eyes flickered toward the opening door, a wave of heat entering with a young man and his daughter. *Dad might not come every Monday*, she told herself. *He's not avoiding me.*

But Wednesday, when she next came to work, she checked the return log, and saw that *The West Wing: Season 4* had been returned under the account of Frank Williamson—a last name she used to share—the day before. She was surprised by the fresh pain that seared her heart; she realized then how hopeful she'd been about seeing him again. Without her permission, fantasies of reuniting with her mom and dad, sharing a meal with them in the home she'd grown up in, had begun forming.

The following Monday, Eileen refused to scan the floor in search of her dad's short-sleeved button-up and khakis, an outfit she assumed he had not deviated from. He was avoiding her. She deserved that.

Behind the check-in desk, she looked up his account. She would take any clue, any hint about the life he now lived without her. His name stared at her from the computer screen in its harsh black and white, much like the man himself, who saw situations plainly with no room for compromise. Her father had been withholding, demanding, but she knew now that her childhood had been a charmed one; she could almost smell the fall days of bike races over crunchy leaves, followed by her mom's roasted chicken.

"Your dad just wants you to make the most of life," her mom would whisper as she tucked Eileen in, her dad's disappointment over a B+ on a science test sending a tear sliding into her hair. Much later in life, Eileen had understood that his high standards were an effort to fill in the chasm that had been left after he'd lost his son. He'd wanted Eileen to live up to the potential that Thomas would never be able to.

She wondered if she had seen that same disappointment in his gaze last week when she'd seen her father for the first time in 14 years.

"I'm taking my break," she said to her coworker Tracy without waiting for an okay; she could feel a tide of emotion rising up as she grabbed her purse from under the desk and headed out into the bright sun.

It was just another injustice that, after a respectable 30-year career as a teacher, the system valued Eileen's contributions so little that her pension wasn't enough for a full retirement. The thought sent a wave of heat through her stomach. She could still see the surprise on her dad's face at finding her behind the library counter.

Eileen found an empty bench near the water fountain where her parents used to bring her and her brother to play. Days she had taken for granted for too long.

"You can be anything you want, Eileen," her dad had told her when she decided to pursue her master's in education at the local university.

"I know, Dad," she'd said, the well-worn argument weighing on her.

"A doctor," he'd offered. "An engineer."

She'd nodded. The truth was, she was afraid of the unknown; she wasn't like her dad, who had left his small town in eastern Kentucky to chase his degree at the state's largest university. She wanted to read books, get married, and start a family with her high school sweetheart. And that's exactly what she'd done, teaching English at the elementary school she'd attended herself, raising her daughter Maddie and eventually having her in class. Frank had always been so proud of Maddie, his only grandchild, a straight-A student.

After nearly a decade of that life, Eileen took up acting at the local theatre as a hobby of her own, much like her own mother had pursued painting. That's where she met Jordan and took him up as well. He was younger than she, full of charm and wit, and brought a carefree spirit to a routine that had become stagnant with Maddie's daily homework and her husband's Saturdays spent at the golf course.

"You're making a mistake," Eileen's dad had solemnly decreed when she brought Jordan to her childhood home, her parents having refused to meet him until the divorce was final. Eileen's dad had been right, of course—able to see the darkness that she couldn't in this man. Eileen had taken this reaction as a personal slight, a framing encouraged by Jordan. Her mom had played the peacemaker, passing messages between father and daughter.

Eileen watched a pair of kids—maybe siblings, maybe not—pounce and scream, playing a game of which the rules were impossible to discern.

Jordan had implemented rules in his new household, which included Maddie half the time. Jordan had begun extracting Eileen's support system with surgical precision. He spoke of Frank and Beverly as though they were overbearing and didn't trust Eileen; he flung insults at Frank when he called the house, such that Frank refused to speak to Eileen at all for a week.

Jordan found a house to buy in the county over, giving Eileen no choice but to teach seventh grade science, a subject she had never taught, at a school she had never stepped foot in, in a community she had never spent time in. The valley between her and her parents had widened to a canyon. They didn't speak for weeks at a time, which turned into months, which turned into years.

Eileen wandered toward the fountain's edge, close enough to feel some of the water's spray, which brought temporary relief from her memories and the summer sun. She'd have to go back to the check-in desk in moments, but tears were forming behind her sunglasses now.

Eileen imagined the dark-paneled walls of that house with Jordan, and instantly felt small and trapped. Maddie had become Eileen's only connection to her parents, to her old life. Maddie visited Beverly and Frank while under her dad's care because Jordan wouldn't allow "his family" to communicate with them. Maddie, a child, would quietly give Eileen updates on her own parents—they were doing well, taking trips across the country in their big new motorhome.

And then, on a cold bright Sunday, Maddie had called her mom and, in a shaky voice, asked her not to pick her up from her dad's; she didn't want to be around Jordan anymore, she'd said. Her sweet 14-year-old girl, making the choice to protect herself—Eileen was miserable but perversely proud of her daughter for drawing a boundary, something Eileen wouldn't be able to do for another decade. Jordan wouldn't allow Eileen to take the issue to family court; now that Maddie was no longer under his control, he had written her off as evil.

Eileen kept up with her daughter's life on social media. Knowing Maddie had a safe place to grow up in Eileen's ex-husband's home gave her a tolerable peace, despite the turmoil of her days spent under Jordan's rule. Maddie was still close with her grandparents, which both compressed and relieved her guilt.

Eileen wiped her cheeks and walked back toward the library, the air conditioning a relief from the sweat now sliding down her back. She was used to sweating, now; she'd taken up running after the divorce from Jordan. It was the only time she felt any sort of clarity.

She regretted so much of her life.

"I'm back," she told Tracy, who'd covered the desk for her.

"Oh good," Tracy said, her eyes scanning the shelves for something. "There's a man here—an older man. He says he wants to talk to you."

It would be too much to wish for.

And then she saw him, her dad, Frank, winding his way toward her, his eyes cast down, his breast pocket full of pens, his steps jangling with loose change like they had since she was a child.

Some things would never change, Eileen thought. But—a hope swelled in her heart—maybe others could.

—KATIE KNECHT (she/her)

The room was silent. The open window let in a soft breeze that ruffled the curtains. Neeya sat alone at her wooden desk, studying her daily scripture. The Lords were generous and kind, but they did not tolerate heretics. Not that Neeya was anything but dedicated. She spent all of her free time dedicated to the Celestials, well, until recently.

The window creaked, and a soft thump told Neeya that she was no longer alone in her quarters. It was always this time of night when she appeared. She was tempted to keep her attention on her studying, but she could feel the eyes on her back, and it made her nervous. And very excited.

The woman on the couch was pale with light purple eyes that glinted even in darkness. Neeya knew that she was tall, much taller than herself at the average, but she looked tiny sitting with her legs bunched up in a comfortable side lean. The one aspect that most made her appear unlike a human was the soft, glowing blue marks along her skin in random spirals, like magical ink had written on her at birth. She wore a royal blue dress with a long, deep neckline meant to draw attention. Sapphires rested embedded along the collar and cuffs at the end of the long sleeves. A mantle of blue and black feathers fell from her shoulders, crested by pauldrons of sharp, jutting obsidian rocks. She sat with her face in the darkness, but below her neck, she was doused in the moonlight that was hers to command.

"Hello, Hekate." She tried to keep the wonder out of her voice. It was not the first time the Goddess had shown herself to Neeya.

"Why don't you join me, Neeya?" Hekate said, ignoring pleasantries.

"I have much to study before Debate tomorrow."

Hekate guffawed, "What better way to study the Celestials than to commune with one?" Neeya could not deny her logic and left her texts to tomorrow. Her anxious enthusiasm increased tenfold with each step towards the couch. She sat beside Hekate, who gave the girl her full attention. "How was your Debate today?"

"You, Goddess of the Night, wish to know how Peasant Acolyte Girl's day was?" Neeya's tone suggested humor, but her soul spoke of flustered bewilderment.

"No, I simply wondered if my advice about *Interpretations of Hekate's Grace* was seen in glorious fruition." Neeya's pride at the Goddess's care faltered, and she wondered if she was like all of the other Celestials: egotistical narcissists, at least according to the stories. Hekate seemed to notice, and said, "My apologies. I meant it as an attempt at humor. Many of Us have not yet grasped it in our separation from humanity. I really was curious about your labors."

The acolyte instantly felt bad about her immediate judgment of Hekate. In all of her visits to her room, she had only ever shown interest in Neeya's life, whether out of an interest in humanity or in Neeya herself, she dared not ask. She promised to be kinder and said, "It went well. Your comments about the Solstice Sheen as seen by the shepherd were well received by the other disciples."

"No doubt thanks to your skill in oration."

Neeya blushed, hoping the darkness would conceal her face. She did not take into account the fact that Hekate's very domain was darkness. Or that she was sitting a mere foot away. "Thank you," she choked out. "I appreciate your visits, for choosing to spend time with me in your divine schedule."

"There is no one else I could conceive to speak with," Hekate did not hesitate to reply.

"But why? I am not unique or interesting." Neeya thought of all the times she shrunk into herself during class and around the temple. If having no enemies meant having no friends, at least Neeya was safe and on a path to simple success in the priesthood. She thought she could live with that. Hekate's interest in her tested her beliefs. She continued, afraid of the Goddess's answer, "Is it because I was the first mortal you spoke to?"

"Does it matter if I choose to be with you?" She had no answer. They sat in silence with only a soft whisper of wind coming through the window. Hekate, always the most comfortable in her own realm, spoke first. "I have a question to ask of you." She waited as Neeya straightened on the couch in anticipation. "I would like to join you as an acolyte, if you will have me."

Neeya expected a dozen other propositions. "What?" Hekate repeated her request to prove Neeya had not misheard. "Would you act as a mortal? The Lords would certainly ask questions."

"Yes, and they are always looking for more minds to persuade, and would they not trust the discretion of an undisputed devotee such as yourself?" Hekate's logic was divine as always.

"Where would you stay?"

"With you, of course," she said softly. She took Neeya's hand and searched her eyes, momentarily flicking down.

The girl hesitated. The idea was tempting, *so* tempting, but her faith told her to be respectful of the divines, and her heart told her to be wary. She pulled away. "I do not know if I can."

"Do you not wish to? Have I made you uncomfortable?" The Goddess was able to inflect genuine sorrow into her holy, omnipotent voice.

"No! It is only, I—I respect you too much." She thought of the feel of Hekate's hand against her skin moments before, and the look in her eyes as she looked at her lips. "It would be like desecrating a temple."

The Goddess of the Moon leaned closer and tucked a stray hair from Neeya's face. She whispered so that even if someone else were in the room, only her intended would catch her words. "There are other ways to worship."

—ASHLEY CAMERON (she/her)

SCOPES

You first spotted Holly at Satan's Hoedown—a monthly, queer, semi-mock, country-music-themed distraction where thrifted cowboy hats and vegan-leather chaps got you half a shot of moonshine before sore ankles the next morning. She was a style-fiend; curly blonde hair under her armpits offset by ruby red lips reflecting a diamond smile in cooling neon. You wore nothing but black, sipping cheap beer and considering her sign, whether anyone could surprise you at that point.

Tia introduced you after Holly tired of the line. Gemini Sun. It made sense considering how effortlessly she intoxicated the space. You clicked right away, which made the next few months beautiful and daunting. Why yes! Holly also ran a horoscope page, but while yours was a witchy takedown of the practice; hers preached positivity to the skies. Holly's following was predominately unemployed, bleached mothers with Etsy accounts, while yours consisted of tattooed space spawn from a forgotten age plummeting to earth after heavy bouts of too much too soon.

"You're a real treat, you know that?" Holly smiled while Dolly Parton sang in the background. "How have I never met you before?"

At that exact moment, you knew the two of you were likely to destroy one another but buried the onset of vibes. "I tend to disappear in crowds," you said.

"Impossible," Holly beamed. "I spotted you right away."

"Well then it must be in the stars."

Three months later, you locked in on a lease and domain name along with an IG account for Simon and Reggie: @TwoFoundFelines. A monthly podcast, *SCOPES*, gathered steam; Holly stirring up controversy with unlikely pairings. You played along out of some reluctant loyalty to your craft, figuring it best to be the voice of reason, even if they were only listening to her

That cringe got you hot, like every cell in your body was on fire, but none could reason with you.

"Hang up your headphones and return to a poignant life of solitude," they'd say. "You're better than this."

You were weak from the flutter and that scared the shit out of you; conversations with Holly often ending in argument or falling off somewhere between orgasm and reality TV binge watch. She always empathized with the worst housewives, chefs, suitors, but you quickly understood why Holly was sitting next you. You were one of the bad ones.

Enter Jay at Tia's housewarming party, just some rando from hot yoga with nowhere to be on a Saturday. Taurus Moon; Holly latched right on, discussing speculative reservations and community outreach. You did shots with strangers; laughed at the soundtrack and threw out a few dance moves, before getting high in the attic with Tia's Christmas decorations. Stoned and ready to go home, Holly and Jay just kept on talking in the living room corner.

You continued like anyone would, speaking your truth into the microphone, posting when your perception felt off.

"But you know Jay had a great idea the other day." Holly smiled at the dinner table. "We should really have them on the podcast."

"Uh huh," you chewed. "Sure."

It went as expected, Holly and Jay subtly pressing your buttons; agreeing passively, aggressively; and synching their chakras without your consent. You refused to argue again after Jay finally left, Holly curling up next to you on the sofa, smitten. "All of that couldn't have gone better today."

"Absolutely," you coughed. "I love that Jay."

How did you always end up in these situations? No matter the person, however beautiful or calm, you'd eventually feel the need to act out, if only to see if they were still paying attention.

It only took a few days for Holly's workload to pile up. She'd just begun two overpriced spiritualism classes: one from a posh influencer in Tibet; the other a Midwest junkie who'd only seen parts of God's inner thigh. You watched a few of their lectures in-between calls at the office. They were trash, but the kind that spoke directly to the camera. "You are worthy of love," they repeated. No degrees in medicine, but just saying the words a certain way qualified them as a professional.

You then made plans with just Jay. They weren't very busy, a little mulching in the backyard when you showed up with a bottle of red wine to say "thanks" for coming on the podcast. It was easy from there: sip lightly and listen, compliment their taste and décor while subtly poking around their brain, making sure they're fully aware of absolutely no arrangement in place. Everything was free and chill on the other side of town.

***

"I can't believe you fucked Jay," Holly wanted to cry, but had gotten so good at turning her emotional imbalances into podcast fuel, she'd nearly forgotten the sensation.

"You're just pissed because I beat you to it."

"You two literally have nothing in common," Holly said. "It will never work."

"Oh, I don't want a relationship," you replied. "I just wanted to make sure you didn't have one either."

"You're so awful."

"You knew that when you met me, but decided to come along for the ride anyway"

"I've always been a terrible judge of character," Holly admitted.

"Typical Gemini."

That night was the last you slept together. It wasn't as good as the first, but a bit better than some of the times in-between. You let Holly keep the apartment and podcast, but had her pay you for the domain name and occasional vet trips for the cats. You unfollowed when it felt right and never thought about that time in your life again. There was always another rodeo in its planning stages, which made the remaining nonsense less daunting. That just came with being born a Scorpio.

—CHRISTOPHER S. BELL (he/him)

Alex searches internet porn for men who look like her ex-boyfriend. Eventually, she finds Jake's doppelgänger; he has brown eyes and pale skin, he even has the same strand of stray hair falling clumsily in front of his face. Alex watches the doppelgänger's facial expressions as he buries himself into his companion. The woman is white and chubby, with floral tattoos on her back. Alex is disappointed the woman doesn't look like her. Alex is a brown woman of mixed ancestry with long, wavy black hair. She has been described as "racially ambiguous" (her mother is mixed Japanese and white, her father is Mexican-American). The doppelgänger's face flushes pink as he nears orgasm. When he turns his face in profile he looks most like Jake. Alex wills the man on her laptop screen to turn slightly to the right—it would make the fantasy so much better, but he's too focused, and far away, and prerecorded to answer to Alex's whims. He tilts his head back and bucks. Alex has an okay orgasm.

She gets dressed and makes coffee. She feels sad and tells herself to stop being so dramatic. She feeds the cat, Arpeggio, and wonders if she should text Jake. She could make it seem like an accident, something like—*Hi! Are you and Chrissy planning on coming camping this weekend? followed by—Oh! Sorry! That was for another Jake. How are you btw?* It's a crap plan, and she adds it to the list of other crap plans she's had in the last month: make macramé plant holders to sell online, move to England to write a novel, refurbish vintage furniture and open a shop on Etsy. She's amazed at her momentary desperation and adds an extra spoonful of honey to her coffee.

At the last minute, Alex decides to call into work—*It's really embarrassing . . . worst case of diarrhea . . . came on so suddenly . . . not sure what it could be . . . actually, I'm so sorry, I have to get off the phone right now.* She's planning on quitting soon.

The last time Alex was at the dentist, she mindlessly flipped through a woman's magazine and read an article with a list of things single women could do to flex their independence—*You don't need a man to have fun!*—Alex imagined a room of lesbians applauding. She ripped the article out and tucked it into her purse. The woman at the front desk glared at her, Alex shrugged her shoulders apologetically.

With the whole day to herself, Alex takes out the magazine article. She'll be like Audrey Hepburn in *Roman Holiday*, brown girl version, without Gregory Peck. She quickly eliminates suggestions like, *Go kayaking* and *Learn an instrument*, she's looking for cheap thrills that don't require a lot of commitment. *Go to a movie.* Alex can't remember offhand the last movie she saw in the theater . . . maybe the Jordan Peele horror movie about the jumpsuit donning tethers. She went with Jake and gripped his thigh the entire time.

She decides to go see an indie film about the unlikely love between an ornithologist and an entomologist called *Feather and Bug.* She buys popcorn and a large soda and meanders into theater eleven, which is completely empty. She sits in the very center of the theater and feels lonely. Alex tells herself to *stop being so dramatic* and eats a handful of buttery popcorn—*what was she expecting for a Tuesday matinee?* Even after the twenty minutes of trailers, Alex is the only person in the theater. Halfway through the movie, Alex has the overwhelming urge to cry. It's not prompted from anything happening on screen—the movie is brilliant and beautiful; it's like watching a still life in motion. The ornithologist has just spotted a yellow warbler. At first, Alex tries to suppress her tears—*what kind of weirdo cries for no reason?* She looks around at the seats surrounding her—red, plush, empty—and finds it impossible to hold back her tears any longer.

***

In her childhood home, there was a large upright wooden piano in the living room, it was the most expensive thing her parents owned, besides their car. The piano was a family heirloom passed down from her maternal grandparents. It was decorated with intricate and detailed carvings—swirling florals and winged cherubs. Alex remembers sitting at the piano, her feet barely reaching the pedals, trying to figure out a song she heard in a movie. Predictably, one of the keys would always get stuck.

After watching an episode of *The Oprah Winfrey Show*, featuring child prodigies, six-year-old Alex imagined herself to be an undiscovered piano genius whose gift had yet to materialize. Looking for a moment of divine inspiration—the correct key played to unlock her dormant talent, she sat at the instrument and played. Her mother yelled from the other room, "Alexandria, would you stop banging on the piano? Too loud!"

In another life she could've been a concert pianist.

***

Jake breaks up with her on a Sunday afternoon. Alex is sitting by the window in their apartment, people watching, and is about to say something funny about the woman with a Pekingese dog in a baby carrier, when Jake says, *Babe, we need to talk.* He says, *It hasn't been working for a long time.* He is talking about their relationship. *I don't think that's true*, says Alex. Jake then commences with a litany of all the things that aren't working (things he has obviously been holding onto); it's really a list of all the things he dislikes about Alex: *You don't have any direction . . . what do you want to do with your life anyway . . . I feel unstable with you . . . if you had some kind of direction, maybe we could make this work . . . I mean, we're not children . . . you don't have any money saved for retirement . . . are you ever going to pay off your debt . . . am I supposed to take care of you . . . it's too much Alex . . . I want a partner, not a dependent.* He says more sentences containing the words "you" and "direction." Alex says, *How's she supposed to network?* Says, *The wage gap!* Says, *Can't you be a little patient . . . I'm figuring it out . . . I swear I'm going to figure it out . . . I just haven't yet.* Says, *I'm not like you, daddy isn't going to get me a job.* Jake starts packing his things.

***

The ornithologist and entomologist are in the Southern Appalachians, it's just gotten dark and thousands of blue ghost fireflies start to appear. The ornithologist says, *I've never seen anything like it.* The entomologist smiles knowingly. They proceed to have a conversation about the seen and unseen, about ghosts, the miraculous and the mundane, the Earth's future, unexplainable phenomena—they are falling in love.

Alex is suddenly struck by the idea that she has always been lonely. Wasn't she lonely when she was dating Jake? Didn't she always feel misunderstood and judged by him, constantly seeking his approval? Jake always kept his love and acceptance at a distance, an unattainable trophy held just out of her reach.

It's like you're waiting for something to happen to you, Jake told her, *you have to make things happen. You want to pretend that you're not responsible for your own life, but you are, you really are.* Was that true? Was she waiting for something to happen . . . for an external cue, or opportunity, or person to come along to tell her what was next? She made decisions every day, from which color lipstick to wear, to which brand of yogurt to buy at the grocery store. It was the big decisions that terrified her, the change-your-life kind of decisions, the can't-go-back-and-change-your-mind kind of decisions—the kind of decisions that smacked with permanence. She wasn't like the characters in *Feather and Bug*, passionate and dedicated to a single calling, she felt aimless and drifting. She was more like the natural world they were studying—wild and migratory—was she, in the end, also trackable, patterned, and predictable?

***

Alex decides to walk home from the movie theater instead of calling a ride. She walks through a neighborhood of townhouses, looks inside the windows, and imagines herself living multiple lives—she's the kind of woman who drinks espresso . . . she's the kind of woman who drinks mineral water only . . . she's the kind of woman who drinks protein shakes . . . she's the kind of woman who drinks whiskey before noon . . . she's the kind of woman with craft-store-art on her wall . . . pop art . . . owns sculptures . . . she's a minimalist . . . a homemaker . . . a career woman . . . a painter . . . a mom . . . she's the kind of woman who spends thousands of dollars on fine art.

Alex walks by a florist and a small antique shop with sun catchers in the window. She is about to walk by a piano showroom, called Crescendo, when she decides to walk in.

The elderly man working is wearing a black beret and says hello. He asks if she's looking for anything in particular.

Alex isn't exactly sure why she is there. "No," she says and skims her fingers across a baby grand.

"Feel free to play anything," says the man and goes back to his computer.

Alex looks at the black piano. It feels enormous and impossible, like staring into the Grand Canyon. She sits timidly. *Who is she?* She presses a C note. It rings out crisp and loud. She plays a chord, the only one she knows. The sound fills her with a deep sense of regret and longing. She plays the keys one-by-one, she plays loudly and the man does not look up; no one tells her to be quiet, no one tells her to stop. She plays a song she's never heard. Alex plays for a long time, watching her fingers dart like fireflies. She plays and plays—and anything feels possible.

—LIZA SPARKS (she/her)

NONFICTION

I was starving. Hungry to the point my metaphorical rib cage was protruding, my cheeks and eyes sunken into my skull. So drained by surface level bullshit. I craved real depth and human connection.

The train tracks a half-mile down the street from my house were looking more and more like maybe if I followed them I'd find the hidden print that lets me opt out of another conversation about the weather or about how Jarred's wife won't sleep with him because he refuses to do a single fucking chore.

"If she had sex with me I'd help out more around the house," he says, like sex is a rewards program.

I want to bash my head against the rust-orange painted wall. Or maybe bash his—watch the red splatter and make the room more lively.

I look at the clock.

There's still 30 minutes left in session.

I'm supposed to have compassion for this. I'm paid to have compassion for this. Lately, I'm just tired of understanding why Jarred won't do the fucking dishes.

My therapist suggested focusing more on my identity as an artist. "Use your writing as an outlet." So I made an Instagram account. Declared: I am an artist. Look at me.

The woman from Australia started following me on Tuesday. I know because I checked her profile four times that day, trying to figure out if she was real or some bot with good taste. When she sent that first message, "your poem about your nervous system mislearning the alphabet gutted me," I read it seventeen times. Screenshotted it. Felt pathetic about it. Did it anyway.

Something about my poems, or maybe about me, made her feel safe enough to send a video of herself reading a poem she'd written. Her Australian accent warmed my ears and made the hibernating butterflies in my stomach shake awake. I must have listened to that video seven times, and honestly, I couldn't even tell you what she said; I was too busy falling for the sound of her voice.

She told me she would date me if I was local.

Suddenly, her beauty wasn't the kind you look at, it was the kind that looks back. The kind that makes your nervous system lean forward before you do.

A young street artist in Sydney who writes poetry. In therapy.

It felt like someone handed me a cheeseburger after months of wet saltine crackers.

There was always paint on her fingers, like she forgot where her hands had been. Always carried a half empty can of something caffeinated. During a video call she gave me a tour of her place, take-out containers lined her windowsills and half-finished paintings leaned in corners like people she forgot.

We spent all of September messaging during the overlap of our time zones. I started waking up at 3 a.m. just to catch her before she slept. I would lie there in the dark with my phone screen making my face blue, watching the dots appear and disappear as she typed. When she was asleep I'd send her snapshots of my day so she could feel like she was beside me on the nature trail—turtles sunning on logs, sandhill cranes picking the shoreline, my feet on gravel, missing hers.

I rearranged my schedule just to talk about how my Mars complements her Venus for three hours.

I was scarfing down every corner of her like a feral cat. I didn't notice that she never asked me any questions.

And when she told me she couldn't swim, I thought she meant in water.

I watched her dart around her house on video calls. The only time she sat still was when she was eating, but even then I could see her body shake from bouncing her legs underneath the table. Always needing a distraction. I knew what this was. The constant movement, the discomfort with stillness. I'd seen it a hundred times in my office. When I gently named the anxiety behind it, she held her palm to the camera "no therapist talk."

I agreed not to psychoanalyze her—that was the first lie.

I spend most of my days reading patterns.

Decrypting things that are said so loudly in the silence. Decoding body language.

There's no magical switch that just turns that off.

Truth is, I refused to see what was so obvious because I was starving.

When you're that hungry, breadcrumbs taste like a feast.

She told me she liked Francoise Hardy, so I listened to *Tous les garcons et les filles* on repeat. She only watched anime, so I binged Frieren and The Apothecary Diaries.

I sent her music she never listened to. She never asked me what I liked.

When October came, she pulled away. I wasn't surprised.

My body shook anyway.

My hands shivering as I typed desperate messages in a bathroom stall, the paint-chipped, green brick holding up my body from collapsing.

The truth is, she was on spring break, she went back to work and no longer needed the distraction from the added silence. She didn't say this of course. What she said was "I don't need to be held to invisible obligations placed on me by someone who expects things I can't provide."

I read that message forty-seven times.

Yesterday, I read it once more.

Tried to parse the grammar. Tried to find myself in it.

Listen, the truth is we don't choose people despite their red flags. We choose them because of the red flags.

I chase unavailable people because if they were fully interested, well, it just doesn't feel like love. Love is supposed to be hard-won. If I'm not chasing, performing, proving—it doesn't register as real. Someone I have to chase feels like home, because home was the place where love was conditional and I got really 142fucking good at performing for it.

My therapist asks: *does this woman remind you of anyone?*

My mother, I tell her. Who loved me most when I was admiring her.

I know my pattern. I can name it with clinical precision.

In grad school they teach you: the opposite of addiction isn't sobriety. It's connection.

What they don't teach: sometimes connection is the drug itself.

And I've always struggled with substances.

—MARTINA SANDORA (she/her)

My body has betrayed me. Broken down by refusing to break down sugar, of all things, turn it into fuel for the day-to-day life I've lived for 55 years. Perhaps its memory is better than mine, though, remembers the time I took in 24 12-ounce cans of Coke in an 18-hour period: 3360 calories, 936 grams of sugar, 1080 milligrams of salt, 816 milligrams of caffeine. Perhaps its math is better than mine, as my actions added up to consequences a 19-year-old couldn't foresee: a surgeon took my gall bladder when I was 32, left me with nothing more than a scar I pretend came from a knife fight when I want to impress myself. Perhaps *betrayal* isn't the right word or emotion; perhaps my body has only lived down to my ideals, carried out my commands as if it were a calculator, maybe even a computer, following lines of code to their inevitable conclusion: garbage in, garbage out.

But shouldn't it subtract, as well, counter the debits with some credits? There are the years of running 100s and 1000s of miles, combinations of 13.1s, even a couple of 26.2s, that should total at least 1 year, maybe 3, maybe more. And those are only when I was an adult. When I was drinking and eating like a teenage boy, I was also running what we called suicides, a term that has fallen out of fashion, thankfully. All of those laps must have lengthened my telomeres, surely.

And so now I sound like a billionaire tech bro who believes that the biblical fourscore and ten isn't already determined by my DNA. They believe they can buy their way to immortality, while I want to outrun death, keep one step ahead of the reaper who surely can't keep a steady pace wearing that robe, carrying that scythe. But all of our bodies break down, find the language of failure, as our cardiacs get arrested, leave us on the side of the road until a skeletal-looking figure arrives in a Cadillac to give us the only ride we're offered, and his gas mileage goes all the way to eternity.

—KEVIN BROWN (he/him)

I've been mourning the fact that I can't seem to write anything revolutionary right now. I feel too content, or too idle, or maybe just numbed by the soft drift of my own life. I can't tell if that's a mercy or proof of a quieter collapse I haven't admitted to. Yikes.

I used to think revolution required a certain torque of suffering—some interior fracture that sparked. These days my fractures feel housebroken, polite little bruises trotting beside me like someone coming home from catastrophe but too well-mannered to complain. So I do what I always do when I feel useless: I go to the café.

An old man who knows the owner walks in with this gentle pomp, like he's hoping the day won't wound him. He orders an oat cappuccino and a Nutella bomboloni, which is basically a pastry engineered to rupture you—joy, pain, depends on your spiritual tolerance.

He sits next to me, pulls out a folded sheet.

A poem. Three lines. A clipped prayer. A ladder shaved down to the nub.

Before I can say, "Please don't read it out loud," he does.

Something about ascending after death.

And I hate, honestly hate, how fast the envy blooms in me. Sharp and tulip-like, pushing through the soil of my chest. Why him? Why this man with sugar dust on his fingers and a casual friendship with the owner? Why does he get the heaven-ladder moment while I sit here feeling like a storage unit full of unused metaphors, climate-controlled and pointless?

Then he mentions, almost offhand, that he wrote it for his brother. Who may not be alright after today.

My envy folds. A blue flame bowing its head.

Outside, snow gathers around a cherry-red VW Beetle—the kind of car someone might name, or kiss the dashboard of. People shake what looks like enchanted pollen from their hair. Somewhere, a brother's veins are running clear with saline while a hospital clock refuses to move. And beside me, the old man bites into his bomboloni.

Chocolate bursts from the pastry like a tiny collapsing star. For the length of a tercet, he curses the sugar stuck under his nails, sweetness insisting on its presence. Meanwhile, his brother's chest is opening to a scalpel somewhere. The jealous poet in me presses a puck of used espresso into a bin. And the universe keeps its indifferent bookkeeping.

Things to do in the land of the dead:
die, apparently
lose your passport
beg a bureaucrat who misplaced a form you never filled out
get a noise complaint
outrun the border guards, somehow.

I insist on the finality of death. The dead do not. They behave like tenants refusing eviction—rattling chains not as omens, but as Yelp reviews about how their bones are arranged. They're not affable pets with detachable jowls.

"Don't you want to know everything about me?" I imagine asking a ghost.
"I sure as hell would," it might say.

Last week, an old incision on my forehead reopened—without fanfare, the way a creek might decide to change direction overnight.

I felt the warmth slide down before I even touched it, and suddenly I was blinking through a bright red curtain. Vision had an on/off switch: blood on, blood off. In the mirror, I looked like someone rehearsing their exit with great sincerity and no talent.

A nurse on the phone asked, "Old blood or new blood?" and I hated that I didn't know. She hated how long I paused. Either way, it slid into my mouth, metallic as a coin pressed to the tongue. Probably old blood, given how unglamorous it looked pooling on the tile, a sad, gelatinous smear.

I walked into the bathroom dripping like I was cataloguing my own execution and pre-cleaning the scene. And yes, part of me wanted it to be dramatically gross, cinephile gross, art-school gross, but also: God, please don't let me shit or piss myself in the grand finale. Who writes the etiquette manuals for dying? Which angel oversees bodily dignity?

The only verb that comes to mind is *spurt*. There should be a glossary for "the moments before the moments before". A diagram. A polite reminder card.

Still, I try to maintain some kind of spectacle. Half the stains in that bathroom aren't even mine; they're ancestral corn-syrup ghosts from the Halloween costume labelled "sexy murder bunny girl." I had Sharpied the tag to make the phrase feel more deranged, serious academic inquiry into trash glamour.

That night, the apartment smelled like cheap vodka leached from plastic cups and the humid breath of everyone trying to be a better, sluttier version of themselves. I'd painted whiskers on too symmetrically, moulded fake blood into a collar, and hopped into the throng with the sincerity of a pilgrim.

Men tugged my tail all night, each expecting something giggly or hollow, a joke with legs. One man didn't tug at all. He leaned in instead, careful, like he didn't want to disturb the orbit of whatever warmth and complication clung to my lower back. His costume, a meticulous Mad Hatter—silk hat tilted, jacket just chaotic enough—made the moment feel like a stage prop and a promise at once. For a stupid, shimmering instant, I let him in. I let sincerity bleed through the latex and sequins, a tiny patch of me unmasked. His hands moved gentle, reverent, and the ridiculousness of it—the absurdity, the theatrics, the perfume of chocolate and fake blood mingling—made it real.

I didn't expect it, but I let him kiss my ass. Slow. Gentle. Respectful in the way that only someone entirely unhurried, entirely present, could be. Everything else—the audience, the costume, the echoes of past performances—fell away. Sometimes all performance is just a pocket of truth punctured by spectacle, a single moment where the ridiculous and the intimate collide. Everybody gets to be sexy, the same way everybody gets to die.

Warhol said something like that—if he didn't, he should have. He had better lighting anyway, and we don't take the same drugs.

Here's a fable instead, because fables outlive manifestos:

A girl grows a wolf-tail in the suburbs—Brampton, Mississauga, Etobicoke, or anywhere that smells like a mall. Teenagers press into each other like mis-shelved books; you can always hear a food court two blocks before you enter it. The girl's tail wiggles on its own, tuned to some cultural nerve that keeps sending shocks. It grows heavier. Hairier. She tapes it to her thigh under Target panties, but it won't submit. It strains. Aspirational. A private biology experiment no teacher will ever grade.

Eventually it drags her down the street—bump, bump—like the wrong end of a chassis towing itself. After a few bodies, she disappears into the tail. It combusts. Lights down. Hidden machinery humming. Everything boiled neat in its slick.

Isn't that adolescence? Grow a part of yourself you can't control. Everyone tries to touch it. Then it burns you from the inside out with its cosmic inventory: dwarf planets, comets, the molten drag of Venus, rubble folding in on itself for one last incandescent day.

A moon that spies on you. Self-help stars. Dust made into prophecy.

Wells. Wheels. Queens and pentacles. Mystery.

"Hands in the well," she tells me when I ask how to serve.

"A lily? A crystal orb?"

"No," she says. "This one's permanent."

The girl would write forever—desert-born, mineral-lovely, all flint and shadow. Language arrives like a winged oracle or a prank wearing a color wheel. A miracle, or something pretending.

"You'll feel liberated," she whispers,
"even if the ice moons keep their distance."

I lost someone in the heat of a cold night. That day's stretched-out light clung to a body close but unreachable. Then darkness: a disciplined lament. In a dream someone made puns for ghosts at the Salon des Refusés. Workers wilted under fate. One believed he could wander off and love a taboo-breaker in a Moroccan field where people carved wooden whistles and cried as a veiled woman prophesied. "Chorus, chorus!" they shouted. He gave up his imagination and became a babe of the abyss.

Everything old and heavy pressed itself into the shape of her words. Desire grew limbs. The body cracked. Someone knelt to worship her footprints.

Myths, dreams, fables, cosmologies—they whirl inside me like I'm a faulty observatory, always off-axis. Meanwhile, Earth keeps happening without permission. We made it deep into the Atomic Age only to discover we're still dragging war like an extension cord through the generations. Families riveted to the conflict of their time. We raise our walking sticks again, staffs of vocabulary. Old torches relighting the shadows.

Night market tonight.

Here's the hinge: things fall apart.
I'm half-asleep, then suddenly on fire.
Undone. Burned. Skinned of all insulation. Raw. Flattened. Doubt-riddled.
Numb in the specific way where you know feeling is outside the door holding
a battering ram.

Rats thrive in sewers, which means technically I'm thriving.
But my dreams lodge formal complaints.

No one notices me. I'm a sewer rat feeling the walls of a labyrinth designed by
the indifferent. Shook. Underdone. Overstuffed and still hungry. Rich rat, poor
rat. Breadline rat. Baker rat. Transformed rat. Stuck-in-a-well rat. Thriving,
technically. Brick-burned. Road-shaped. Milepost. Sign.

Maybe mourning the absence of revolution isn't about lacking fire—it's about
not knowing where the fire actually is. Not about being speechless, but
suspecting the world padded your throat. A slow cosmic recalibration of a self
that keeps changing shape faster than the language meant to hold it.

And still, in the café, the old man licks chocolate off his fingers.
His brother waits in the trembling corridor between survival and not.
Snow burrows into the red Beetle that couldn't care less about metaphysics.
Sugar dissolves under fingernails.
Somewhere, a wolf-tail drags a girl forward.
Somewhere else, a prophecy hums with its wings closed. Somewhere I touch
my forehead again, waiting for old or new blood to tell me what story it wants.
Maybe revolution isn't cinematic, but quieter: a tercet over a cappuccino, a
pastry collapsing into sweetness, a fable refusing extinction, a rat navigating
the underground map of a city. Maybe revolution is just the sum of ruptures:
bursting, spilling, leaking, burning, growing, dragging, propelling—the small,
stubborn machinery of staying alive.

Maybe my envy isn't dramatic, just a small tool the world places in my hands.
A compass made of pulse and petal, its needle trembling toward whatever
warmth remains. A tulip pushing through unsettled ground doesn't call itself
desire; It just rises, trusting a center it's never seen. Maybe I'm no different.

I thought I wanted revolution. What I have instead is this: an ungainly,
luminous patchwork of the living world. A cosmology not built of grand
proclamations, but of the ordinary disorder that keeps happening anyway.
Death misplacing its paperwork. Blood muttering as it dries. Myths slipping
back into the room like patient spiders. And an old man reading me a poem

about a brother who may or may not survive the afternoon, his voice catching right after the word after.

It's all smaller than revolution—and also infinitely larger.
The world scattering signs like seeds, asking only that I notice.

And maybe that noticing is its own quiet pivot toward the molten center of what I still want—the place where the living keep gathering, unruined, for one more day.

—MARIE ANNE ARREOLA (she/her)

ABOUT THE CONTRIBUTORS

✳ **Andrew Rader Hanson** is a poet and photographer, who lives in South Florida. In his free time, he lifts weights, hikes, practices languages, and reads widely. His work has been published by *Spectrum Literary Journal, Pembroke Magazine, The Hong Kong Review* and more. He was also nominated for a BOTN award and the Scottie Merril Poetry award. "You Can Build It" (Ghost City Press) is his most recently published chapbook. He workshops poetry with the Vivian Laramore Rader Poetry Group which he co-founded.

✳ **Anna Nguyen** abandoned her PhD studies and decided to rewrite her dissertation in the form of creative non-fiction as an MFA student at Stonecoast at the University of Southern Maine. She blends literary analysis, science and technology studies, and social theory to reflect on institutions, language, expertise, the role of citations, and food. She is currently pursuing a second MFA in poetry and fiction at New England College and also hosts a podcast, *Critical Literary Consumption.*

✳ **Ashley Cameron** (she/her) holds a Bachelor's in English from Arizona State University. She loves to write short stories in various genres, especially fantasy, sci-fi, and horror with touches of romance. She aspires to be a Young Adult novelist and video game writer, hoping to bring vivid worlds and relatable characters to life. Her work can be found in the online literary magazines *Outrageous Fortune, Normal Noise, The Orange Rose, Canyon Voices,* and *Quirk* as well as in "Tempe Writes: An Anthology, Volume 10."

✳ **Ashley Parker Owens** (she/her) is a poet and student of mystical traditions living in Kentucky. She holds MFAs in Creative Writing from Eastern Kentucky University and Visual Arts from Rutgers University. Her previous poetry collections include *Euphoric Drift* (2018), *Retrospecter* (2019), *Unruly Spirits* (Dancing Girl Press, 2018), *Puppet* (Rinky Dink Press, 2018), and *Territorial Misfortune* (2017).

Learn more at www.ashleyparkerowens.com. Visual Poems www.youtube.com/@visual_poems

✳ **Bianca Ambrosino** (she/her) is a somewhat reclusive poet from Richmond, Virginia. Her unique, Autistic perspective illuminates universal themes with startling connections and vivid synesthesia. She spends her time writing, raising her children, and reading countless academic papers/ scientific publications (for fun).

✳ **Brian L. Jacobs PhD.** (he, they) is a poet and editor of *Tofu Ink Arts Press.*

✳ **Cassady O'Reilly-Hahn** is a poet with an MA from Claremont Graduate University. He is an editor for *Foothill: A Poetry Journal* that highlights graduate student voices. He works for Deluxe, a company that localizes TV and Film for a global audience. In his free time, Cassady writes Haiku for his personal blog, orhawrites and his Instagram @cassady_orha. Cassady currently lives in Redlands, California, with his wife, Anabelle, and their two pugs, Wyatt and Jasper.

✳ **Christopher S. Bell** is a writer and musician. His shorter work has appeared in numerous publications in the previous decade. His latest music project, H088Y_FARM, may just be the best mess you've never heard. He currently resides in Pittsburgh, Pennsylvania.

✳ **Ciara Louise** has adored (been abnormal about) writing ever since she could hold a pencil. She prefers to write prose but occasionally delves into poetry.

✳ **Cryptid Parke** earned their bachelors degree in creative writing and editing & publishing from Pacific University Oregon. Growing up in the Midwest instilled Cryptid with a fierce love of the strange and lonely, and they can now be found leaving ghosts of themself in every place that they visit. Cryptid can be found on Instagram @cryptidparke and their work can be found on their website: https://cryptidparke.carrd.co

✳ **Devon Webb** (she/her) is an autistic writer & editor based in Aotearoa NZ. Her award-winning work has been published extensively worldwide & accumulated seven Best of the Net/Pushcart nominations. She is currently working on her debut poetry manuscript & a publishing initiative advocating for grassroots community collaboration & spiritual consciousness. She can be found online at @devonwebbnz.

✳ **Ella B. Winters** (she/they) is a double immigrant, writing from the South-East of England. She is a social worker, currently working on her PhD in Health Sciences. Her work often explores themes of identity, memory and belonging. Instagram: @ella.b.winters

✳ **Emelia Delaporte** (she/her) is a recent graduate of Virginia Tech, where she studied English. In her time at the university, she served as editor-in-chief of *Silhouette Literary & Art Magazine*. Her work has been published in the *Silhouette, the Shenandoah Avalon* and the *Floyd County Moonshine*, as well as featured at the Giovanni-Steger Poetry Prize. She currently lives, works and creates in Virginia.

✳ **GJ Welsh** is a poet, author and copywriter from the humble, dusty dirt roads of the Eastern Cape along the coast of South Africa. He is currently residing in Karachi, Pakistan, where his newborn baby just screamed his way into the world. He is soon to be published in *Ulramarine* and *Bright Flash Literary Review*. His work has received the Cannes Lion, Clio Awards and the Loerie Awards. His writing treads the fine line between mythology and reality, always with a strong sense of humanity.

✳ **Jenny Benjamin** is the author of the following novels: *This Most Amazing* (Armida Books), *The Terrian Trilogy* (Ananke Press), and *Heather Finch* (Running Wild Press). Over forty of her poems have appeared in journals and magazines. She has published three poetry chapbooks: *More Than a Box of Crayons* and *Painted Women in the Walls* (Finishing Line Press) and *Midway* (No Chair Press). Her poetry collection, *THIS BLUE WORLD*, is forthcoming with *Finishing Line Press*.

✳ **Julietta Bekker** (she/they) is a writer and educator who lives in Portland. Their poems have been published by *Pile Press, Oyster River Pages, Seedlings, Bitten Melon Review, Gather, Flat Ink Magazine, The Dread Literary Review, The Inflectionist Review* and *Querencia Press*, among others.

✳ **Julio César Villegas** was born in San Juan, Puerto Rico—raised in Essex County, New Jersey. Immigrants are beautiful, borders imaginary.

✳ **Kate Horsley** (she/her) is a creative writing lecturer whose first novel was shortlisted for the Saltire Award. Her second was published by William Morrow. Her short fiction has appeared in magazines like *The Cincinnati Review, The Citron Review, Fictive Dream, BULL, Paragraph Planet, Blood+Honey, Tiny Molecules, Flash Fiction Online, SEXTET, Ink, Sweat, & Tears, Fish Barrel Review, Cake,* and *Strix,* and placed in competitions including Bath, Bournemouth, Bridport, Oxford, and Smokelong.

✳ **Katie Knecht** is a native Kentuckian back in her hometown after 11 years in NYC. She earned her MFA in creative writing from Manhattanville College and works as a copywriter for a tech company. She has been published in *Montana Mouthful, Scribble, Wraparound South,* and more. She particularly enjoys petting cats and eating ice cream. Find more on her website: katieknecht.com and read her weekly newsletter: katieknecht.substack.com.

✳ *Island of Wak-Wak Press* (Orebro, Sweden) recently released **Ken Anderson's** *The Ward at Twilight: Goth Poems*, nominee for the Elgin Award. *Red Ogre Review Books* (L.A.) released his *The Goose Liver Anthology* (Mother Goose Meets Edgar Lee Masters' Spoon River Anthology), also a nominee for the Elgin Award. His first poetry book was *The Intense Lover. Coffin Bell Journal* nominated his poem "Blood Quartet" for the Best of the Net anthology.

✳ **Kevin Brown** (he/him) teaches high school English in Nashville. His fourth collection of poetry— *Jack Imagines a Different Map*—is forthcoming from Finishing Line Press in May 2026. He also has a memoir, *Another Way: Finding Faith, Then Finding It Again*, and a book of scholarship, *They Love to Tell the Stories: Five Contemporary Novelists Take on the Gospels*.

You can find out more about him and his work on social media sites at @kevinbrownwrites or at http://kevinbrownwrites.weebly.com/.

✳ **Kiersten McMonagle** (she/her) is a Philadelphia-based writer. She's been writing since she learned to hold a pencil, with her recent work focusing on the balance between her queer identity and her upbringing in the Catholic Church. She can be found on Instagram @Kiersten_McMonagle.

✳ **Levi Abadilla** is a queer Filipino author who grew up in the Cebu province, and who enjoys all things weird and uncanny. Their work has been featured in *Hominum Journal, Singapore Unbound*, and *Black Fox Literary Magazine*. More of their work can be found on leviabadilla.wordpress.com. When not writing, they can be found hanging out on their Bluesky (@escapedscp).

✳ **Liza Sparks** (she/her) is a writer, poet, and creative. Her work is informed by her intersecting identities as a brown-multiracial-neurodivergent-pansexual-woman. Liza is a student in the 2025-2026 Poetry Collective at The Lighthouse Writers Workshop in Denver, Colorado. Her work has appeared or is forthcoming in *Allium, CALYX, TIMBER, Split This Rock, Pangyrus LitMag, The Morgue, Black Fox Literary*, and many others. Liza is a Pushcart Prize and a Best of the Net nominee.

✳ **Marie Anne Arreola** (She/her) is a cultural journalist, editor, and writer from Sonora, Mexico. She is the founder and editor-in-chief of *PROYECTO VOCES*, a digital magazine amplifying emerging voices across art, literature, music, and design. Her work—featured in *Latina Media Co., Hypermedia Magazine, Lucky Jefferson*, and other outlets—explores identity, memory, and grassroots cultural practices throughout the Américas.

✳ Six states, a B.A. in English and MFA in Writing later, **Mark Fleckenstein** settled in Massachusetts. A Massachusetts Cultural Council Grant recipient, twice nominated for a Pushcart Prize, he's published six poetry books and three chapbooks: *The Memory of Stars*, (Sticks Press, 1995), *I Was I, Drowning Knee Deep*, (Sticks Press, 2007), & *Memoir as Conversation* (Unsolicited Press, 2019).

✳ **Martina Sandora** (she/her) is a queer therapist-turned-writer whose work focuses on longing, attachment, and the ways we chase connection when we're starving for safety. She is based in Illinois.

✳ **Maxwell Bauman M.F.A.** (he/him) is the Associate Publisher and Managing Editor of Ben Yehuda Press, the Owner and Editor-In-Chief of *Door Is A Jar Literary Magazine*, a print and digital publication now celebrating its 10th year, and the Lead Editor of *Aggadah Try It*, an imprint of *Madness Heart Press*. He is a contributor to *Chicken Soup for the Soul*. Maxwell is He is the author of Jewish horror short story collection *The Revised Anarchist's Kosher Cookbook* and the novella sci-fi/ fantasy *The Giant Robots of Babel*.

✳ **Mikayla Elias** (they/them) is a writer from Nashville, Tennessee living in London, England. Their prize-winning work has been featured in anthologies worldwide, such as *Waxing and Waning Lit* and *Samfiftyfour*. They are the contributing editor of the zine "re:animated" and the author of the collection "bending toward the light." When they aren't writing, you can find Mikayla at the nearest karaoke bar.

✳ **Molly Rose Strugatz** (she) is a writer, artist, and teacher from Brooklyn, living in Barcelona. A graduate of the Jack Kerouac School of Disembodied Poetics, her work explores community, nature, and folklore. Her writing has appeared in *Parabola, Tummy Ache, Blue Marble Review, Adult Groceries,* and elsewhere. Her written and visual work have been published and exhibited internationally.

✳ **Niamh Cahill** is a poet and essayist from Montclair, NJ. A recent graduate from Kenyon College, she received distinction for her Creative Writing Senior Thesis and served as Editor-in-Chief of the college's first and only chapbook press, *Sunset Press*. Her work has appeared in *Spires Magazine, ONE ART, Discretionary Love, The Eunoia Review,* and *Grub Street Literary Magazine*. She loves Adrienne Rich and her dog.

✳ **Nicholas Olah** (he/him) has self-published four poetry collections and his work appears or is forthcoming in *Humana Obscura, Thimble Literary Magazine, Wildscape Literary Journal, Boats Against the Current, Shadow and Sax,* and more. Olah is a 2x Pushcart Prize nominee and his poem, "On the Drive Home", won third place in The Poetry Lighthouse Prize in spring 2025. Check out more of his work on Instagram at @nick.olah.poetry.

✳ **Richard A. Quiroz** is a Librarian from South Texas who loves to read and write when time permits. He enjoys visiting museums, historical sites, and other places of interests which holds memory that is still very much present.

✳ **Rowan Elliot Gibson** is a lifelong reader and writer who dreams of publishing their own weird, queer books someday. They are currently studying for a Master's in Library and Information Science with plans to become a public librarian. They have one cat named Noodle, more than enough books, and many queer beloveds.

✳ **Sam Moe** is the author of eight books. Her most recent poetry collection, *RED HALCYON*, is forthcoming from *Querencia Press in* 2026. Her debut short story collection, *I MIGHT TRUST YOU*, is out from *Experiments in Fiction* (2025). She has attended the Sewanee Writers' Conference and received fellowships from the Longleaf Writer's conference and the Key West Literary Seminar. Sam has also attended residencies at The Writers' Colony at Dairy Hollow, VCCA, and Château d'Orquevau.

✳ **Satori** (she/her) is an author, poet, teacher, and community activist based in Chicago. Her work explores themes of identity, belonging, and transformation, drawing inspiration from her experiences growing up brown and queer in Upstate New York, generational trauma, the immigrant experience, and love in all its forms. *Monsters, Clowns, & The Holy Fool,* her debut collection of poetry and prose, was published by *Raging Opossum Press* in October, 2025.

✳ **Shivani Gupta** (she/her) is a writer, curator, dancer & researcher. Her first chapbook *my mother is a mixed metaphor* was published by Rockwood Press in 2026. Her work has also featured globally in *BBC, Forbes, the Edinburgh Fringe Festival, Baby Teeth Journal, Ranger Magazine, Tiger Leaping Review* & more. She is a current In-Surreal-Life fellow & serves as the Development Committee Chair for the Chicago Poetry Center. She loves sauces, baked goods & all round silliness. Website: https://shivanigupta.space/

✳ **Shraddha Shah** (she/they) is a neuroscientist, writer, and organizer concerned with questions of trauma, diverse intelligences, complicities of the academy, and tries to embody anti-imperial and anti-colonial liberatory modes of being. Her writing explores questions of bodies and belonging and how we situate ourselves individually and collectively in liberatory struggles. As an organizer, they co-founded and runs ZinesforFalastin and Gaza Writers Series, to amplify voices of indigenous Palestinian artists through creating and promoting zines of their work. Her writing has appeared in We The Soil, Revolute, Houston Chronicle, and Mondoweiss.

✳ **Stephanie Valente** (she/her) is a poet, copywriter, and the author of the collection *Internet Girlfriend*, published by Clash Books. She is at work on a novel. She lives in Brooklyn, New York. @stephaniemariavalente and https://stephanievalente.substack.com

✳ **Sylvia Godreaux** (they/them) is a Maine based poet and artist. Although they are still finding their place in the literary world, Sylvia is very active in their local writers' community, and was featured in Querencia Press's Spring 2025 anthology. Sylvia uses their art to explore their struggles with physical and mental health, their experience living in a queer and marginalized body, as well as trauma, abuse, nature, and everyday magic. They can be contacted at sylviagodreaux@gmail.com.

✳ **Tatiana Samokhina** (she/her) lives in the beautiful suburb of Surry Hills and works in the bustling City of Sydney. She is an English teacher and fiction translator, in love with literature. Her work has appeared in *Elegant Literature, 3 Elements Review, Jokes Review, Australian Writers' Centre*, and more.

✳ **Thyrsa Rheya** (she/her) is a Belgian writer, who loves horror stories but would never watch a horror movie. She has (platonically) fallen in love with short stories because of Stephen King, Haruki Murakami and Koji Suzuki. She got third place in a horror writing contest on Scribophile. She loves animals and dislikes fusilli.

✳ **Topher Shields** (he/him) is a queer poet from Aotearoa New Zealand exploring hau (breath), ritual, and memory. *Black Cotton Gospel (1999)* reimagines his own youth on Karangahape Road and recalls Hape, whose calling out (karanga) from the ridge gave the road its name—a breath that still carries. His work appears or is forthcoming in *Puerto del Sol, The Shore, The Bangalore Review,* and *Cathexis Northwest Press*, tracing the sacred through queer lineage, myth, and the body's remembered song.

✳ **Vanessa Pedroza** (she/her) is a punk-loving, quiet-tongued misfit with a phoenix-burning beat in her chest. Words are her breath, but her eyes tell her soul best. She'll tip-toe the veil to the shadow world to place her ear upon the universes' heartbeat. When she isn't breaking ancestral curses & piecing broken parts into collages, she is dipping her toes into the sun-burnt dirt imagining worlds beyond this one. You can collect her cascade of teeth on Instagram @mouth.wound

✳ **Whitney McShan** (she/her) is a Texas native who lives outside of Austin with her wife and son. Her work has been featured in *Hellbound Books Anthology of Horror, Instant Noodles Lit Mag, Radical Publishing's With Teeth, Dug Up Magazine, and more.* She is interested in the strange, the uncanny, and the monstrous. Find her at instagram.com/whitney.mcshan

✳ **Zac Gosney** (he/they) is a writer from the shittiest part of North Carolina. He thanks you for your time.

9 781963 943528